RO

THE OUTSIDER

by

MELINDA METZ

POCKET PULSE
New York London Toronto Sydney Singapore

This book is a work of fiction. Although the physical setting of the book is Roswell, New Mexico, the high school and its students, names, characters, places, and incidents are either products of the author's imagination or are used fictitiously. Any resemblance to actual events or locales or persons, living or dead, is entirely coincidental. P8 0 L 89

POCKET PULSE published by
Pocket Books, a division of Simon & Schuster Inc.
1230 Avenue of the Americas, New York, NY 10020

Copyright © 1998 by POCKET BOOKS,
a division of Simon & Schuster Inc.

First published in 1998 byArchway Paperbacks

ISBN: 0-671-77466-2

First Pocket Pulse printing November 1999

10 9 8 7 6 5 4 3

POCKET PULSE and colophon are trademarks of
Simon & Schuster Inc.

Printed in the U.S.A.

"One Sigourney Weaver and one Will Smith." Liz Ortecho slid two thick burgers onto the table—one with avocado and sprouts, one with jalapeño peppers and cheese.

Then she waited. The customers in the booth were obviously tourists. And every tourist who came to the Crashdown Cafe had at least one question about . . . the Roswell Incident.

"So is your family from around here?" the guy in the *Lost in Space* T-shirt asked. The blond woman sitting across from him flipped open a battered notebook and stared at Liz.

"Yeah," Liz said. "My great-great-great-grandfather inherited a ranch outside town. My family's been in Roswell ever since."

The woman uncapped her pen. The man cleared his throat. Here it comes, Liz thought.

"So did any of your relatives ever tell you any stories about, you know, the UFO crash?" the guy asked.

These two were a total trip. I bet they have every episode of *The X-Files* on tape, Liz thought.

"Well . . ." Liz hesitated. "I guess it would be okay to show you." She pulled a worn black-and-white photo

1

out of her pocket and gently placed it in front of them. "A friend of my grandmother's took this picture at the crash site—before the government cleaned it up."

The two tourists leaned over the blurry photo and studied it carefully.

"Whoa," the woman mumbled. "Whoa."

"This looks exactly like the alien from the autopsy video," the guy exclaimed. "Same oversized head and small, hairless body. I've got to get it on my Roswell Incident web site." He reached for the photo.

"You'd be dead by the end of the week." Liz snatched the photo away. "Just because it's been more than fifty years since the crash doesn't mean the air force wants the truth exposed. They still want everyone to believe that weather balloon story they used as a cover-up," she explained.

Liz glanced around the cafe nervously. She wanted to make sure her father wasn't in earshot. If Papa heard her telling this story, he'd rip off her head and feed it to her for breakfast.

"I shouldn't have shown this to you. Just forget about it, okay? You never saw it." Liz rushed back behind the counter.

Maria DeLuca shook her head, sending her blond curls flying around her face. "You are *so* bad."

"Hey, they'll have a great story to tell when they get home. And I'll have a great tip," Liz answered.

Maria sighed. "You and your great tips. I've never known such a money-hungry waitress."

Liz shrugged. "You know how I feel. I need as much money as I can get because—"

"One day after grad it's *adios* and *hasta la vista*, baby," Maria interrupted. "I know, I know. You're not going to spend your life in a town that has two movie theaters, one bowling alley, one lame-o comedy club, one even more lame-o dance club, and thirteen alien-theme tourist traps."

Liz had to smile. Her best friend did an almost perfect impression of her. "I guess I say that a lot, huh?"

Maria grabbed a dish towel and started wiping down the counter. "Only ten times a day since fifth grade," she joked.

"If I didn't have five thousand relatives watching me all the time," Liz said, "maybe I could have some fun once in a while."

She sighed, imagining a life where she didn't have to worry about doing something—anything—that would make her large, loving extended family worry about her future. She was the first daughter in her family headed for college, and her family wanted to make sure that she stayed on track. And not turn out like her sister, Rosa.

Liz pulled a handful of change out of her pocket and dumped it on the counter.

"Wow," Maria said. "Great tips. Maybe I should get my own picture of a baby doll someone left out in the sun too long." Maria scrunched up her nose. "Though I don't know if I could do that whole 'you'd be dead by the end of the week' thing without cracking up."

"Just practice in front of the mirror. That's what I did," Liz told her.

3

"It would take a lot of practice," Maria complained. "Everyone always knows when I'm lying. My ten-year-old brother is a better liar than me. The guys my mom goes out with never believe *me* when I say how nice it is to meet them."

Liz snorted. "Big surprise." She popped open the cash register and traded her change for bills. Thirty-three more dollars for the Hasta la Vista Fund. Thirty-three seventy-three, actually.

The opening notes of the *Close Encounters* theme played as the cafe door swung open. Max Evans, tall and blond, with killer baby blues, and Michael Guerin, dark and intense, ambled over to the corner booth in the back. Both were students at Liz and Maria's high school.

"Of course they sit in *your* section," Maria grumbled.

Liz and Maria each covered six of the cafe's flying-saucer-shaped booths. They divided the dining room in half from front to back so they each got a couple of booths by the windows. Those were the most popular.

"You get the tourists and the cute guys, and I get those two," Maria continued. She jerked her chin toward the booth nearest the door. "They're having some big fight. They just scowl at me every time I get near them."

Liz glanced at the two men in the booth. One was big and beefy. The other was smaller but muscular. They were leaning across the table toward each other, talking intently. She couldn't hear what they were saying, but they both looked furious.

"I think you deserve a good table after dealing

4

with those guys. You can take Max and Michael," Liz volunteered.

Maria narrowed her blue eyes. "Okay, what's going on?"

Liz wrapped her arm around Maria's shoulders. "You're my best friend. Can't I just do something nice for you out of the goodness of my heart?"

"Nope." Maria shrugged Liz's arm away. "I repeat—what's going on?"

"Nothing," Liz insisted. "I just feel like taking a little vacation from all the testosterone junkies."

Maria raised one eyebrow. "Translation, please."

"Guys," Liz explained. "I'm so tired of their . . . guyness."

"All guys aren't like Kyle Valenti, you know," Maria told her. "Take Alex. He's totally cool."

Alex Manes *was* totally cool. Liz could hardly believe she and Maria had only been friends with him for a year. She felt as if she'd known him forever.

"You're right. Alex is the best. But he doesn't count."

Maria frowned. "Why not?"

"'Cause he's *Alex*," Liz said with a shrug. "He's not a *guy* guy. Not like Kyle. You should have seen Kyle after school today. He will not accept the fact that I won't go out with him again. He actually got down on his knees and followed me down the hall with his tongue hanging out, begging. All his friends were watching, laughing like the idiots they are."

It made Liz wish she knew karate. She could have really given his friends something to laugh about.

"How romantic. And that classy move didn't

5

convince you to go out with him again?" Maria's voice rose in fake shock.

"Uh—that would be *no*. And I'm not going out with anyone else for a while, either," Liz declared. "I'm going to stay home, rent chick flicks, take bubble baths, and wear comfy old sweatpants."

Liz was looking forward to it. To be fair, most guys she'd been out with—not that there had been that many—weren't losers like Kyle Valenti. Kyle actually had thought Liz would *enjoy* sitting next to him on the couch watching him play Nintendo. He hadn't even offered her a turn!

But even with the other guys, there had just been that "sameness" about them.

"My love life is pathetic," Liz mumbled. "I just need some time to myself, for myself."

"Well, I can mix you up some great herbal bath oils," Maria offered. "But if you stop dating, there are going to be some very unhappy boys at Ulysses F. Olsen High."

"Like who?" Liz demanded.

Maria glanced over at the booth where Max and Michael were sitting. "Max Evans," she said.

"Max?" Liz repeated. "Max is my buddy. He's not interested in me like that."

"Oh, please," Maria shot back. "How could he not be interested? You look like some kind of Spanish princess or something with your long black hair and your amazing cheekbones. And let's not talk about your skin. Do you even know the word *zit*? Plus you're smart and—"

Liz held up both hands. "Stop!"

Maria was the most loyal person Liz knew. If you were her friend, she stuck by you no matter what. And Liz and Maria had been friends since the second grade, when they bonded over a hurt baby bird.

"Okay, I'll stop," Maria answered. "But believe me, Max Evans is more than interested. He probably has the words *Property of Liz Ortecho* tattooed on his chest. Max—"

"Hi, Michael!" Liz said loudly as Michael walked up to the counter. She hoped he hadn't heard any of their conversation.

"Hey." Michael raked his fingers through his jet black hair, making the top even more spiky. "I was wondering if you had a job application I could fill out."

It was hard for Liz to picture Michael working in the cafe, busing tables and making change and stuff. It seemed too normal, too ordinary for Michael. He should have a job as a Navy SEAL or something like that. Michael was always joking around, but there was a definite edge to him.

Liz reached under the counter and pulled out a pad of forms. "We don't have any openings right now. But I'll talk to my father, and as soon as something comes up I'll have him call you."

"Oh, I think you're going to be having some openings real fast," Michael answered in a serious tone. "Unless your dad likes waitresses who stand around gossiping instead of waiting on tables." He winked.

Maria threw her dish towel at him. Michael cracked up.

7

"I'll go," Maria said. She picked up two menus and followed Michael over to his booth.

Liz shot a quick glance over at Max—and found herself staring directly into his bright blue eyes. They were such an unusual shade, strange and beautiful. Not the blue of the sky or of the ocean.

Max held Liz's gaze for a second, then he looked away.

Maria wasn't right about Max—was she? Liz had known Max since third grade. He had been her lab partner since they were sophomores. But they never hung out outside of class. And Liz hadn't picked up on any vibe signaling that Max wanted to be more than friends.

Liz grabbed the nearest napkin holder and restocked it. What would it be like to go out with Max? He wasn't really her type. He was quiet. And kind of a loner.

He saw the world in a different way from most people. He said things that made Liz stop and think. Like when those scientists in Scotland cloned that sheep. A lot of people talked about who they would clone if they could—scientists or athletes or movie stars. But Max was more interested in whether or not the soul could be cloned—and if it couldn't, what that meant. Spending time with Max definitely wasn't boring.

Liz wiped a drop of milk off the counter. She moved the ketchup bottle up a fraction of an inch so it was exactly even with the mustard bottle. Then she stole another peek at Max.

8

No one could say the boy was homely, that was for sure. If there were a beefcake calendar of Ulysses F. Olsen High hotties, Max would be in it. Tall, blond, buff, with those blue, blue eyes . . .

Liz felt her face get hot. It was weird thinking of Max that way. Most of the time she forgot he was certifiably gorgeous. Max was just *Max*. She couldn't—

"I don't want the money tomorrow. I want it now!"

The angry voice interrupted Liz's thoughts. She jerked her head up and saw everyone in the cafe staring at the men in the booth by the door. The beefy man clenched and unclenched his fists as he glared at the muscular man.

I'd better go get Papa out of the office, she thought. Their argument looks like it's about to get ugly.

Liz turned toward the door marked Employees Only.

"He's got a gun!" Maria screeched.

Liz spun back toward the dining room. Her heart slammed against her ribs. No. Oh no. That's all she could think. Over and over.

The muscular man held a gun to the beefy man's head. "You won't need any money if you're dead," he said. His voice was calm. Calm and cold.

Click.

The muscular man cocked the gun.

Liz wanted to run, she wanted to scream for help, but she was paralyzed. Her mouth refused to open. Her legs refused to move.

The beefy man gave a howl of fury. He launched himself across the table at the muscular man.

9

An eardrum-shattering explosion rocked the room.

Liz flew off her feet. She hit the wall behind her, then slumped to the ground.

She felt something warm and wet gushing across her stomach, soaking into her uniform.

"There's so much blood," Liz heard Maria cry.

But she sounded so far away.

So far . . .

Max sprang up from his seat in the booth. Instantly Michael grabbed him by the arm and jerked him back into his seat.

"Let go of me," Max cried. "Liz could be dying. What are you doing?"

"No, what are *you* doing?" Michael tightened his grip on Max's arm. "Are you planning to heal her in the middle of a restaurant? Why not just send the government an invitation—hi, I'm here, why don't you come on over and get me?"

Michael was right. Healing Liz would attract attention—a lot of attention. But if he let Liz die when he knew he could save her . . .

That was just not an option.

"I'm willing to risk it," he told Michael.

"*You're* willing to risk it. But what about me? What about Isabel?" Michael demanded.

Max stared down at the table. He didn't answer. He couldn't answer. He would risk his own life for Liz. But how could he risk the lives of his sister and his best friend?

"If the government has proof that one of us

exists, they'll know there are more. They won't stop searching until they find us—*all* of us," Michael continued.

"I can't stop the bleeding!" Maria screamed from behind the counter.

Max's heart slammed against his ribs. Liz was dying! He bolted to his feet. "I'll think of something. I promise," he said in a rush.

Before Michael could stop him, Max raced to the counter and vaulted over it. Pain filled his heart as he stared down at Liz. He swallowed hard.

Maria held a thick towel over Liz's stomach. But nothing could stop the blood pouring from the gun-shot wound.

Max heard Liz's father on the kitchen phone, giving the cafe's address to the ambulance. They're going to be too late, Max thought. He knew it. He could see it.

The halo of color surrounding Liz was usually a warm, rich amber that made Max wish he could wrap himself up in it. But now her aura had turned a dull, muddy brown. And it was growing darker by the second.

Darker and darker as her life force drained out of her.

Every person's aura was different, as unique as a fingerprint. But the only time anyone's aura turned black was at the moment of death.

Max pulled Maria out of the way, trying to ignore the tremors of fear racing through her body. He wanted to comfort her, but he didn't have one second to spare.

He knelt beside Liz and placed his hands over her wound. In an instant his fingers were slick with blood.

I love her. The thought exploded in his mind. It was true. He'd been keeping it a secret, even from himself. Loving a human wasn't smart. It wasn't safe. But he couldn't help it. He loved Liz, and he would not let her die.

"Let me through!" he heard Liz's father yell from behind him. "Let me see her!"

Max didn't move. He didn't answer. He had to focus on Liz now. Liz was the only thing that mattered.

He closed his eyes and began drawing deep, even breaths. Trying to make the connection.

Think about Liz, he ordered himself. Anything about her.

The way her hair always smelled of jasmine. The way a dimple appeared in her left cheek when she smiled. The way she loved to tell stupid alien jokes. The way she listened with total concentration when he talked to her.

Ahhh. He almost had it. He almost had the connection. He just needed to get a little closer. . . .

"The ambulance is almost here," Michael muttered behind him.

Max took another breath.

Images flashed into his mind, coming so fast, Max could hardly register one before the next appeared.

A stuffed dog with a chewed-off ear. A Mr. Wizard junior chemistry set. A blond little girl holding a baby bird. An onrushing car. Liz at about age five in a pink dress covered with cupcakes. A valentine. The high dive of a large swimming pool. Max's own face.

And he was in. Connected.

He could feel the blood gushing out of Liz's body as if it were his own. Feel her breath in his own lungs. Hear the sound of her heartbeat in his own ears.

First the bullet, Max told himself. He focused his attention on Liz's body. On *their* body.

Yes. There it was. He could sense the exact position of the bullet. Of the lead. Of the molecules of lead.

Then he *nudged* the molecules. That's the only way he could describe it. He nudged them, and they broke apart. The bullet dissolving into microscopic particles. Harmless now as they were swept away in Liz's bloodstream.

"The ambulance is pulling up out front," Max heard Michael say.

But he sounded far away. So far . . .

Max focused on Liz's somatic cells. The cells of her body. Of her stomach. Of her muscles and tendons. Of her skin.

And instead of nudging he *squeezed*. Squeezed with his mind. Urging the cells closer together. Healing.

Max felt hands on his shoulders, shaking him. "You've got to disconnect. Now, Max," Michael ordered. "The ambulance crew is coming through the door."

And he was out. Separate again. Alone again. A wave of coldness washed through him, and he shivered.

Max slowly raised his hands and stared down at Liz's stomach. Under the blood her skin was whole and perfect. He released a shaky sigh of relief.

Liz opened her eyes and stared at him. "I . . . you . . ."

13

"I'll explain everything later," Max whispered. "But now I need you to help me."

He grabbed a bottle of ketchup off the counter and smashed it against the floor. He dumped the contents over the blood on Liz's uniform.

"You broke the bottle when you fell," Max told her. "Okay, Liz? You broke the bottle when you fell, that's all."

A man and woman dressed in white jumpsuits hurried behind the counter. "Everyone move aside and give us some room," the woman paramedic instructed.

Max backed away. Did Liz even understand what he'd asked her to do?

Liz struggled to sit up. "I'm okay," she said. Her voice sounded hoarse. "When I heard the gunshot, I jumped. Then I fell. I . . . I broke this ketchup bottle and spilled ketchup all over myself."

She held up the broken bottle so everyone could see it.

Then Liz looked straight at Max, her dark brown eyes melting with emotion. He felt his breath catch in his chest.

"I'm okay," she repeated.

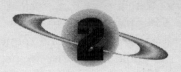

Liz couldn't stop staring at Max. He gave her a tiny smile, a private smile meant only for her. What did you do to me? she thought. How . . .

Her brain felt like it was humming, vibrating at a really low frequency. It was hard to think.

The paramedic knelt down in front of Liz, blocking her view of Max. No! Liz thought, struggling to stand up. She needed to keep Max in sight right now. It made her feel . . . safer.

Lying on the floor, she'd had the feeling of rushing away, being *forced* away from the cafe, from her father and Maria—from everything and everyone familiar. And somehow Max had brought her back.

"Don't try to move yet." The paramedic grasped Liz firmly by the shoulders.

Liz tried to focus on the story she was supposed to tell. She brushed her fingers across the front of her uniform, then held her hand up so the woman could see it. "It's ketchup, just like I told you. I know it looks like blood, like a lot of blood. . . ."

And there is blood *under* the ketchup, a lot of blood, she thought. I was bleeding to death. I was dying. A shiver rippled through Liz. She wrapped her arms around herself, but it didn't help. She still felt cold.

"I know it's ketchup—I can smell it. I'm getting the urge for a big plate of fries," the woman joked. She pulled out a tiny flashlight and shone it into Liz's eyes. Then she took Liz's wrist in her hand and checked her pulse.

"Is she okay?" Mr. Ortecho asked. He was blinking superfast, the way he always did when he was about to lose it.

Liz felt a rush of protectiveness for her father. He had been devastated when Rosa overdosed. For days after the funeral he had lain on the sofa covered by a red afghan—even though it was the middle of summer. And no matter how many times Liz had gone into the room, she'd always found him in exactly the same position.

He must be terrified, she thought. I'm the only child he has left. She wished this had happened on his day off.

"I'm fine, Papi," she answered. She heard a tiny tremor in her voice, but she thought she'd done a good job of sounding normal. Except for the fact that she had called her father Papi. She hadn't used that name since she was a little girl.

"I didn't ask you," Papa snapped. "Are you a professional? No. You don't know if you're fine or not."

"I'm the professional, and I say she's fine, too," the woman answered. "I thought she might be in shock. I'd be in shock if someone shot at me. But she's just fine." The woman glanced over her shoulder at her partner. "Guess we should head out."

16

"Thanks." Liz pushed herself to her feet. Her father wrapped her in a hug so tight, her ribs hurt. "Let's not tell Mama what happened, okay?" she whispered.

"Are you kidding? There's no way your mother's radar would miss this. The second one of us walked in the house, she'd know something was wrong." He gave a choked laugh as he released her.

Liz scanned the cafe, searching for Max. She had to talk to him. She had to find out what he did to her. But he was gone. So was Michael.

Max had sounded so intense when he asked her to lie for him, like it was something really critical. If anyone took a close look at the floor, they would know her ketchup story couldn't be true. The spatters of blood on the tile floor looked bright red and shiny slick—not tomato red and clumpy.

"I—I'd better mop up the ketchup. Someone is going to slip." Liz rushed over to the corner and rolled the big yellow bucket over to the red stains. She drenched the floor with dirty gray mop water.

"I'll do that," her father said. He pulled the mop out of her hands.

"Come on. Let's go to the ladies' room and get you cleaned up," Maria said, slipping her arm through Liz's.

"Good idea." Liz didn't know how much longer she could stand here acting calm and talking about ketchup.

She turned toward her friend. Maria's face was pale. Her peachy pink blush looked way too dark now. It stood out on her cheeks in ugly splotches.

Before Liz could take a step, the front door of the

cafe swung open and Sheriff Valenti strode in. The heels of his boots echoed on the tile floor as he made his way up to the counter.

Everyone at Olsen High knew Kyle's father. He did a locker search practically every week. He stopped anyone under eighteen who was driving even one mile over the speed limit. He showed up at practically every party, checking to see if there was any underage drinking going on.

"I got a report that there were shots fired at this address," he told Mr. Ortecho. "Can you tell me what happened?"

He's going to ask a billion questions, Liz thought. What if he doesn't believe the ketchup story? She felt her heartbeat speed up.

"I was in my office. I heard two men yelling, then a shot," Mr. Ortecho answered in a shaky voice. "I ran out and saw my daughter . . . I saw my daughter lying on the ground, bleeding."

"It was ketchup," Liz said quickly. "The gunshot scared me. I jumped back, then I fell. I broke this ketchup bottle, and it spilled all over me."

Valenti turned toward her. "Is that right?" he asked. He took off his hat, and Liz could see the red band the brim had made across his forehead.

"Uh-huh," Liz answered.

Why did she feel so intimidated? He'd asked the question in a calm voice—he didn't yell or anything. And it wasn't like he was some big, powerful-looking man. He was about average height, not much taller than Liz.

But there was something about him. If Liz had to pick one word to describe Sheriff Valenti, it would be *deliberate*. She got the feeling that his every word, his every gesture was calculated. And if he was so careful about what *he* did and said, he must scrutinize every detail about other people.

Did he notice how wet the floor is? she thought suddenly. Does he wonder why we mopped? It *was* kind of a bizarro thing to do three seconds after someone tried to shoot at her.

Valenti didn't ask another question. He just stood there.

Did he believe her story? Liz wished she could see the sheriff's eyes. But he hadn't removed his mirrored sunglasses. All she could see in them were reflections of her own face.

"Two guys in that booth over there were having a fight," Maria put in. "One was sort of short but not scrawny, more muscular, and the other one was a big beefy guy."

"That's right!" Liz agreed. "They were fighting about money, I think. Yeah, about money."

You're babbling, Liz told herself. Just slow down. The more you say, the easier it will be for Valenti to catch you in a lie.

Valenti raised one eyebrow. "And then what happened?"

"And then one of the guys—the short one—pulled out a gun. The other guy tried to take it away from him, and the gun went off," Liz answered.

"I'll need to get a description of both of them."

Valenti pulled a little notebook out of his pocket.

Liz forced herself to laugh. "Definitely," she said. "The guy with the gun had shaggy brown hair. He was about five-nine, maybe a hundred and eighty pounds."

"Mustache, tattoos, anything like that?" Valenti asked.

"I don't think so." Liz glanced at Maria for help. Dealing with the sheriff was making her nervous.

"I don't remember anything, either," Maria added.

"What about the other guy?" Valenti tapped his pencil against the notebook.

"Taller," Maria answered. "Maybe six-two. And bigger, with a beer belly."

Valenti jotted down notes as Maria continued her description. In a few more minutes he'd be out of there. And Liz could find Max.

"I guess that's it," Valenti said. "I just have one more question—where's the bullet hole?"

The bullet hole? Oh, my God, Liz hadn't thought of that. "Uh, it must be in the wall." She turned around and pretended to search for it.

Valenti leaned across the counter. "Don't see anything," he said.

Liz could feel his breath against her ear. He was giving her the creeps. Valenti has no way of knowing you're lying, she reminded herself. She turned back to face him and shrugged. "Maybe I was so freaked out when I saw the gun, I just imagined it went off."

"Well, the mind can play tricks on you—especially when you're under stress," Valenti answered.

Yes, he's buying it, Liz thought.

"But your father heard the gunshot, too," Valenti commented. "And so did the woman who called in to report the shot."

I didn't think of that, either. I'm totally losing it, Liz realized. I have to just shut up. "I don't know what to tell you," she said. "Do you mind if I go clean up? This ketchup is really sticky."

"Go ahead," Valenti answered. "I know where to find you if I have any more questions."

"Come on, Maria." Liz grabbed her by the arm and pulled her over to the ladies' room. She led the way inside and shut the door behind them.

Liz scooped her hair up and gathered it into a big Pebbles Flintstone ponytail on the top of her head. She reached into her pocket, pulled out a scrunchie, and used it to anchor the ponytail in place. Somehow she could always think better when all her hair was out of her face. Stupid, but true.

Maria rolled out a long sheet of brown paper towel and held it under the cold water. Then she wrung it out and handed it to Liz. "So, do you want to tell me why you lied to Valenti and everyone else?" she asked.

Liz froze with the paper towel halfway to her stomach. She could feel water dripping onto her shoes. "I wasn't lying," she answered, but her voice sounded high and fake.

Maria looked at her for a long moment. "Yeah, right." She pulled a dish towel out of the side pocket of her uniform. "The red stuff on this isn't ketchup. It's blood. Your blood, Liz. I was holding the cloth over

21

your stomach, and I felt the blood soaking into it."

Her voice cracked. Tears glistened in her eyes. "I pressed down as hard as I could, but it wouldn't stop. You were dying, Liz. I was watching you die."

Liz grabbed the edge of the sink with both hands. She suddenly needed help standing up. When Max asked her to lie for him, Liz had just turned off her emotions and done what he wanted. It was like she had formed a big glass bubble around herself, keeping all the fear out so she could deal with her father, the paramedics, and Sheriff Valenti.

But Maria's words blasted a hole in the bubble. I almost died, Liz thought. The words repeated themselves in her head again and again. She sank down to the floor and leaned against the wall.

Maria sat down next to her. She wrapped her arm around Liz's shoulders. "It just hit you, didn't it?"

"Yeah," Liz admitted. Her throat stung, and her eyes filled with tears.

"So tell me."

Liz pulled in a long, hitching breath. "Max healed me. It's impossible, but he did. I heard you screaming. You sounded really far away. Then I guess I blacked out or something."

It felt good to say it out loud. It made her feel less crazy. "The next thing I remember is feeling hands pressed against my stomach. Warm hands," Liz continued. "That's all I felt—no pain or anything. I looked up, and I saw Max."

"Wow. I just . . . wow. He saved your life."

"Yeah, he did," Liz answered. But she didn't quite

believe it. It was like a dream or something, seeming less real with every passing second. How could Max have healed a gunshot wound? "He told me to lie. He said he'd explain everything—then he disappeared."

The smell of ketchup mixed with drying blood wafted up from Liz's uniform. She felt a wave of nausea. She stood up and soaked another paper towel, scrubbing frantically at her uniform until the towel started to fall apart.

Maria joined Liz in front of the mirror. She wiped her eyes and gave a shaky laugh. "This is supposed to be waterproof mascara."

"I don't think they've invented tear-proof stuff yet." Liz tore off a strip of paper towel and handed it to Maria.

Maria's eyes widened. She leaned toward Liz. "Liz, you shouldn't even bother trying to get the ketchup out," she said, pointing to the fabric. "You'll have to burn that uniform or something. Look."

Liz looked down and saw a small round hole in the cloth. She felt her stomach turn over. That's where the bullet had gone in. That's the bullet hole Valenti had been hoping to find—and only some blobs of ketchup kept him from spotting it.

"You're right," Liz said slowly. "I have to burn this. And that cloth, too." She took the blood-soaked dish towel out of Maria's hand.

Maria kept staring at the bullet hole.

"I can't believe there was really a bullet inside my body." Liz wrapped her hands protectively across her stomach.

"Move your hands a second," Maria said. "There's something weird. It's like your skin is shining."

Liz lowered her hands. The patch of skin underneath the little hole did look kind of strange—almost silvery. What was going on?

She slowly unzipped the front of her uniform. When she looked down at her stomach, she began to feel light-headed.

This wasn't happening. None of this could be happening.

But there, on her stomach, were two iridescent handprints. Melded with her flesh. Max's handprints.

Isabel Evans pulled out her top dresser drawer and tossed the contents into the center of her bed. Okay: lips, eyes, skin, nails, scent, she thought. She snatched up every lipstick, lip gloss, lip balm, and lip pencil she saw and piled them in the upper-right-hand corner of her mattress.

Then she picked out all the eye shadows (cream and powder), all the eyeliners (liquid and pencil), all the mascaras, and all the eyebrow pencils. She heaped them in the upper-left corner of the bed, then added two eyelash curlers and a bottle of Visine.

Max always teased her when she did this. He said Isabel was like a little kid dividing her Halloween candy into categories—plain chocolate, chocolate with nuts, hard candy and licorice. But organizing her makeup and stuff calmed Isabel down whenever she was upset. And she was upset now. No, *more* than upset. Totally panicked and heading toward hysterical.

24

If her brother didn't get home soon, he'd never get the chance to tease her ever again—because Isabel would kill him. And Michael, too.

One of them had used a lot of power—healing, dream walking, *something*. She could feel the power crackling in the air—all the tiny hairs on her arms and the back of her neck were standing up. And the smell of ozone drifted in through her open window— the same way it did after a thunderstorm.

That meant something was very wrong, because Max and Michael never used their power just for kicks. And whenever Isabel did—which was a lot because using her powers was *fun*—they both always chewed her out.

Something big must have happened. Something that made her brother and her friend risk breaking their own rules. But that wasn't the scariest part. The scariest part was that she had felt a burst of terror from both of them. Not fear. *Terror.*

Isabel couldn't read Max, or Michael's thoughts. But she could feel their feelings, always. Most of the time she tuned them out. Who wanted to feel Michael's annoyance over some argument with his foster parents or Max's sappy pleasure when Liz Ortecho smiled at him?

But there was no way to block the terror coming from both of them right now. It would be like trying to ignore a volcano erupting in the middle of town, spewing lava everywhere.

Isabel scooped up blushes, and moisturizers, and concealers, and foundations (liquid and powder). She shoved them over to the lower-right-hand corner of the bed. She started to add an apricot-and-oatmeal facial scrub, then hesitated. Should she do cleansing stuff separate this time?

She couldn't think straight. Where were Max and Michael? They had to know she would be going crazy.

Isabel threw the facial scrub in the trash. She hated the way it felt on her skin, all gritty and itchy. She shouldn't have bought it in the first place.

She heard a car pull up in the driveway. Finally! Isabel bolted out of her room, down the hall, and out the front door. Max and Michael were striding up the front walk toward her. Max avoided looking her in the eye, and Michael's face was set and grim.

This is bad, Isabel thought. This is very bad. "Where have you guys been? What happened?" she demanded. Her voice sounded high and shrill.

"Inside," Max answered as he brushed past Isabel.

"Inside," Isabel muttered. She and Michael followed Max into the house. Isabel slammed the door shut behind them. "Okay, we're inside. What is going on?"

"Are Mom and Dad home?" Max asked, ignoring her question.

"No, this is their Clovis day," Isabel answered impatiently. Mr. and Mrs. Evans had decided to expand their small law practice once Max and Isabel started junior high. Now they kept offices in Roswell and over in Clovis, about an hour's drive to the northeast.

Max nodded, then headed into the living room, with Michael right behind him. "Don't you walk away from me," Isabel cried. "I want to know what you did.

And don't tell me nothing—I felt the power jolt. It practically knocked me off my feet."

Her brother didn't answer. Max flopped down in the recliner. He rested his head on the Indian blanket tossed over the back, his face gray and pasty looking next to the vivid reds, golds, and greens.

He was freaking Isabel out. Max loved to take charge. He loved telling her and Michael what to do. And now he wouldn't open his mouth.

Isabel turned to Michael. "You tell me. Right now."

"The saint used his powers to heal a gunshot wound—and he did it in front of witnesses," Michael spat out. He sat down on the nubby brown sofa, then stood right back up. He was obviously too wound up to stay in one place.

"A gunshot wound? Are you crazy?" Isabel screamed at Max. Then she glared at Michael. "He's your best friend—why didn't you stop him?"

"I tried," Michael shot back. The expression in his gray eyes warned Isabel to back off.

"Did the police show up?" Isabel asked, her voice rising higher and higher.

"Valenti was pulling into the parking lot as we were pulling out," Michael answered.

Isabel's stomach clenched. Sheriff Valenti scared her. She did everything she could to avoid him. If he crashed a party, Isabel made sure she was out the back door. If he showed up at school, Isabel made sure she was quietly studying in a corner of the library. And now Max had practically handed the guy an invitation to come after them.

"Did the witnesses get a good look at you? Do you think they'll be able to give Valenti a decent description?" Isabel asked.

"They'll probably be able to give him names and addresses," Michael muttered.

Isabel gave Max The Look, the "tell all—or else" look.

"Liz Ortecho is the one who got shot. She knows I did something to heal her. I think her friend Maria DeLuca knows, too," Max admitted. "She must know. She was the one trying to stop the bleeding."

"That means Valenti is going to be at our door in, like, two seconds," Isabel cried. "He's going to find out the truth about you!"

"Izzy—," Max began.

"And it's not going to take a genius to figure out that if you're not from around here, your sister isn't, either," Isabel went on. "How could you do that to me, Max? Valenti will know the truth about both of us. He'll turn us over to some government agency, and—"

"I think we should get out of here," Michael interrupted. "I think we should get in the Jeep and start driving, and I don't think we should stop until we're out of the state."

"Stop. Just stop it, okay?" Max ordered. He sat up a little straighter and shoved his blond hair off his forehead. "Liz lied to the paramedics for me. I told her to say that she broke a bottle of ketchup and spilled it all over herself, and she did. We can trust her. And I'm sure Maria will go along with Liz."

"You don't know that," Isabel insisted. "You put all of us in danger, Max."

28

"Now you know how I feel every time *you* use your powers," Max shot back.

"No. Do not even try to make this about me," Isabel yelled. "You—"

"Liz is going to have a lot of questions," Michael cut in. "What exactly are you planning to tell her?"

"The truth," Max answered.

"No way!" Michael exploded.

Isabel stared at her brother. She recognized the expression on his face—he had made up his mind.

Slowly she sank down on the arm of his chair. She had to find a way to make him really hear her. She had to convince him he was about to do something that could destroy them all.

"Max, we're not living in Disneyland, okay?" she said quietly. "We aren't living in a happy, perfect place. It would be nice if we were, but we're just not. You can't trust everyone. It's not safe."

Max shook his head. "I'm not talking about *everyone*. I'm talking about Liz."

"Liz and probably Maria," Isabel reminded him. "You think you know them, but there is no way you can possibly know how they'll react when you tell them you're—not the same as them. They might look at you and see something totally repulsive and scary."

Max didn't answer. Isabel could see that he wasn't convinced.

She stood up and began to pace. Maybe Michael was right. Maybe they *should* just take off. They weren't safe now that two humans were so close to learning their secret.

29

"You're the one who made the rule, Max. You made us all swear we would never tell anyone, remember?" Michael asked.

Isabel could hear the strain in his voice. He sounded almost as scared as she felt.

"And you were right," Michael continued, "because there are humans out there who would track us down and kill us if they found out we exist."

Isabel heard a car pull into the driveway.

She spun to face Max. "It's happening," she spat at him. "Valenti's coming after us already. What are we going to do?"

Max sprang out of the recliner and rushed down the front hall. He took a quick look out the thin window next to the door. "It's not Valenti, it's Liz," he told Isabel and Michael.

Isabel slumped against the wall and closed her eyes. Max felt a pang of worry—he'd never seen his little sister so hysterical before. But he didn't have time to deal with her now. He had to concentrate on Liz.

He swung open the door before Liz rang the bell. She jumped in surprise but quickly recovered. She stared him straight in the eye. "You said you'd explain everything later. It's later." Liz crossed her arms and kept looking at him. Obviously she wasn't leaving until she'd gotten an explanation.

Max sighed. He knew Isabel and Michael were probably ready to assassinate him, but what else could he do? Liz must be more freaked out than all of them— she'd almost died.

"Come in," he told her, ignoring Isabel's groan. "Let's go into my room. Michael and Isabel were about to . . . watch a video."

Michael and Isabel didn't say anything to back Max up. They didn't say anything at all. They just stared at Liz. If they could, they would be shooting death rays out of their eyes right now, he thought. Lucky for Liz, that was one power they didn't have.

Max led the way into his room and closed the door.

"Uh, sit down. Do you want something to drink or anything?" Max grabbed an armful of dirty clothes off the floor and hurled them into his closet. "We have soda, and juice, and these power drink things Isabel likes, and probably some other stuff."

"No, I'm okay." Liz sat down on the bed.

Max started to sit next to her, then changed his mind and leaned against his dresser. He'd fantasized about having Liz Ortecho in his bedroom, playing out every possible variation. But he'd never imagined a situation like this.

"So," Liz said. She fiddled with the braided silver bracelet on her wrist.

"So," Max repeated.

Liz's aura had grown lighter. But it hadn't returned to its usual warm, rich amber. It was a sickly yellow. What is it going to look like after I tell her the truth about me? he thought. Is Isabel right—will Liz see me as some repulsive mutant creature?

If she did, who cared about the rest? Who cared if he was captured and experimented on? Nothing could be worse than Liz looking at him and seeing something hideous, something to be feared.

Max knew he had to say something soon but didn't know how to begin.

Liz twisted her bracelet around and around. Man,

she's got to be nervous enough without me standing here staring at her, Max thought.

"So, um, how are you feeling?" he asked.

How are you feeling. What a dorky thing to say, he thought.

"I'm still sort of shaky, I guess," Liz answered. "That's normal, right? I probably have all this adrenaline racing around in my body with nothing to do. Like I drank too much coffee—"

"Yeah," Max said. "When I was a kid, I almost got hit by a car. My heart didn't quit pounding for, like, an hour. I was riding my bike. I don't know how old I was, but I was still the age where clipping playing cards to the spokes was considered cool, so—"

"Max, let's just stop. We're both totally babbling," Liz interrupted. She took a deep breath, then continued. "I lied to everyone just like you asked me to. But I need to know what really happened."

"Okay. You're right. No more babbling. No babbling allowed from here out. No—"

"Max!"

"Okay, okay. But before I start—there's no chance I could get *you* to believe that ketchup bottle story, is there?" he asked.

Liz gave a short laugh. "I don't think so." She pulled her shirt out of her jeans.

What was she doing? Max's mouth went dry. He struggled to keep his expression neutral.

Liz slowly slid up the shirt, revealing the skin of her stomach. Max released his breath in a hiss when he saw the two shining silver handprints. *His* handprints.

33

"I didn't get these from a ketchup bottle," Liz said. She reached out and took one of his hands in hers. Max held completely still. What should he do? What did she *want* him to do?

Liz met his gaze for a long moment, then she drew Max's hand toward her stomach. She matched Max's hand to the silver print, carefully positioning each finger.

Can she feel me trembling? he thought. When he was healing her, Max had been totally focused on dissolving the bullet and closing the wound. But now . . . now he was hyperaware of the texture of Liz's skin, soft and smooth. So warm underneath his palm.

Max sat down next to Liz. She kept his hand pressed against her stomach. "You did this, Max," she said, her voice charged with emotion. "You saved my life. How?"

He slowly removed his hand. Liz dropped her shirt back down.

"I don't know how to start," he admitted.

"Just tell me. Whatever it is, just tell me," Liz said.

This is Liz, Max reminded himself. They had been in school together since the third grade. If Max had to pick one human to tell the truth about himself, he would choose Liz. She really cared about things, about people. So do it, he thought.

"You know I'm adopted, right?" he asked.

"Uh-huh." Liz waited.

"My parents, my real parents, are dead."

"Oh, God, Max. That's awful," Liz answered. "I didn't know. Do you remember much about them?"

Typical Liz. She'd already forgotten all about herself, about the questions she wanted answered. Now she was totally focused on him.

"I don't remember them at all. I wish I did," Max answered. "But I think . . . I think I inherited the power to heal, the power I used on you, from them."

Liz started to respond, but Max rushed on. If he didn't keep going, he was afraid he'd never get it out.

"My parents died in the Roswell crash. They . . . they weren't human. And neither am I. That's why I can do things like, you know, heal. With my hands."

There was a long, uncomfortable pause. Liz inched away from Max on the bed. When she finally spoke, her voice sounded way too calm.

"I don't know what you want me to say," she said, not meeting Max's eyes. "Should I start with the fact that the UFO crash supposedly happened more than *fifty* years ago—and you're only a senior in high school? So your parents have been dead longer than you've been alive?"

She didn't believe him. Max had never even considered the possibility that she wouldn't believe him.

"There were incubation pods on board, and—," Max began, but Liz didn't let him finish.

"Or maybe I should just skip ahead to the really big problem with your story—there *was* no Roswell crash. Every scientific investigation has confirmed that."

Liz stood up and put on her jacket. "You know, I thought you trusted me. I thought you were going to tell me the truth." Her voice was cold, and ugly crimson splotches had appeared in her aura. Max had never seen her so angry. [1]

He blew out a sigh of frustration. He'd been so focused on how Liz would react when he told her the truth that he hadn't stopped to think she might not believe him. Who *would* believe him? It was like saying he was the child of the Loch Ness monster or something.

He had to find a way to convince her. If Liz walked out of here feeling like he'd been jerking her around, Max didn't know what she'd do. She might even decide to tell Sheriff Valenti what had really happened at the cafe.

"What about Colonel William Blanchard?" Max blurted. It was the first thing that popped into his head. "He was the commander of the army airfield. The guy was in charge of an atomic bomb squad strike force, so he had to be pretty well respected. *He* made the announcement that a flying disk was recovered."

"I really don't want to have a world's-greatest-unsolved-mysteries kind of conversation with you right now," Liz snapped. "You promised me you would tell me everything, and you're obviously not going to do it."

She turned toward the door.

"I would never lie to you, Liz," Max said desperately. "Let me prove it."

"Fine. You have two minutes. Prove it."

He jumped up and grabbed her hand. Liz jerked away, but Max held tight. "You said you wanted proof," he reminded her.

"Okay," she murmured warily.

Max began rubbing her bracelet, concentrating on

36

the molecules of silver. He gave the molecules a little *tap* with his mind. He wanted them to move apart, but not too much. Just a little more, he thought. He gave the molecules another tap and felt the bracelet turn to liquid under his fingers.

Liz gave a tiny gasp as the bracelet began to drip off her wrist. The metal melted faster, sliding to the floor in a silver stream. It formed a circular puddle at Liz's feet.

"I was telling you the truth, Liz," Max whispered. "I swear."

Liz stared down at the silver pool, then raised her eyes to Max's face. "I . . . I have to go." She slowly backed toward the door—as if he were some vicious animal that might attack if she moved too quickly.

Max felt his throat close up. She's looking at me like she doesn't even know me, he thought.

"Liz, wait!" he begged.

She moved faster. "I—I can't," she said. "I just . . . can't."

Max was frantic. He had to find a way to fix things. He couldn't let her leave like this.

Quickly he reached down and plunged his hands into the silver puddle, molding it in his hands, pushing the molecules back together. When the bracelet was re-formed, he held it out to Liz.

Take it, he thought. Please just take it. All you have to do is move one step toward me.

Liz opened her mouth, then closed it. She turned and bolted out the door.

Max stared down at the bracelet in his hand. He

slowly walked over to his dresser and pulled open the bottom drawer. He gently placed the bracelet all the way in the back and covered it with clothes.

He didn't want to see it again. He didn't want any reminder of the way Liz had looked at him when she finally understood what he really was.

Liz tried to put the key in the ignition, but her hand was shaking too hard. "Come on, come on, come on," she whispered. She didn't want to be there if Max decided to follow her.

She used her other hand to help guide the key into place and started the engine. The car gave a little jerk as she pulled out onto the street.

When she reached the corner, she turned left instead of right. She would go straight to Maria's. She couldn't deal with going home yet. Her parents would start fussing over her, and Liz was afraid she'd just blurt out everything to them.

Her mother would probably insist she go to a doctor or something. And Papa was a total law-abiding citizen—he didn't even jaywalk—so he would make her call Sheriff Valenti and tell him exactly what happened. Liz wasn't ready to do that.

She didn't know *what* she wanted to do. Thinking about Max made her brain freeze up, like a computer trying to download a file that was way too big.

Liz made another left. She'd driven to Maria's so many times, she could do it on autopilot. She picked up speed as she headed down the street.

Stop sign, she told herself as she approached the

intersection. Stop sign! But the message didn't get from her brain to her foot fast enough, and she drove straight through. She heard a car horn give a long, angry honk behind her.

"Sorry," Liz whispered. "I'm sorry, I'm sorry." Tears filled her eyes, blurring her view of the road in front of her. Drawing in a shuddering breath, she swerved over to the curb and stopped. Her heart pounded in her ears. It was beating so hard, she could feel it in her fingertips as she clenched the steering wheel with both hands. She slowly let out her breath.

Okay, just calm down, she thought. Maria's house was only a few more blocks away. Liz checked the rearview mirror; she checked the side mirror; she looked over her shoulder and checked her blind spot. Then she slowly started back down the street.

She concentrated on driving the same way she had the day she took her driver's test. She made sure she stayed exactly at the speed limit, not one mile slower or faster. She came to a full and complete stop at the next stop sign. She clicked on her turn signal early enough—but not too early—when she reached Maria's street, and she did a perfect parallel-parking job in front of Maria's house.

Made it, she thought. She climbed out of the car and hurried up the front walk. She rang the bell, waited one second, and rang it again.

"I could have used you two minutes earlier," Maria said when she opened the door. She led the way into the living room, still talking. "My mother just went out on a date looking like some rock star. I told her she should change, but of course she wouldn't listen to me. Maybe if you had—"

"I talked to Max," Liz interrupted.

"You look awful," Maria exclaimed. "I'm sorry. I didn't even notice—I was in total rant mode. What happened? What did he say?"

Liz sat down on the overstuffed couch. There was no good way to tell her, so Liz just blurted it out. "He said he was an alien."

Maria giggled.

"I'm serious."

Maria giggled louder. "Does . . . does he have antennae?" she asked, cracking herself up. She plopped down on the couch next to Liz and rocked back and forth, her shoulders shaking with laughter.

Liz waited. When Maria was in one of her laughing fits, she was pretty much unstoppable.

"Did he let you see his laser gun?" Maria laughed so hard, she snorted, which made her laugh even more. Her cheeks turned red, and tears stood out in her eyes.

Finally she noticed that Liz wasn't laughing, too. "Oops. I'm sorry." She gave one last giggle. Then she sat up straight and blotted her eyes with one of the couch's little throw pillows. "Tell me what really happened."

"I just did," Liz said. She rushed on before Maria could start laughing again. "Think about it. You said yourself that I was about to die, that blood was pouring out of me. Max healed me. He closed up the wound just by touching it. What human could do that?"

Maria stared at Liz in astonishment. *At least she knows I'm being serious,* Liz thought. "I know it sounds crazy. I thought Max was jerking me around when he told me that. I thought he was just handing me a totally lame story.

"But then he touched my silver bracelet, and it melted."

Maria's eyes were wide and frightened.

"Do you know how hot silver has to get before it melts?" Liz asked, her voice rising. "Nine hundred and sixty-one degrees Celsius. And the bracelet didn't even get hot. It didn't even feel warm. It's impossible! It should be impossible—but Max did it." She broke off, rubbing her wrist. There wasn't a red mark or anything where the bracelet had been.

"I . . . I think we need some of my special antistress tea," Maria said. She stood up and headed toward the kitchen without another word.

Liz followed her. "Are you okay?"

"Uh-huh. Yeah. Definitely." Maria grabbed the copper teapot and carried it over to the sink. She turned on the water and let it run into the pot until it spilled over the sides. Maria stared at it, her eyes blank.

Liz took the pot away from her. "Let's just sit down. We're both a little too freaked to be using major appliances."

"You're right." Maria slid into a kitchen chair, and Liz sat down next to her. "So what do we do now?"

"I don't know," Liz answered. "I don't know where to start. It's not as if I can go on-line and do research on the culture and beliefs of aliens from Max's planet.

I mean, I don't know if they—if Max's . . . species—just want to live here with us, or if they want to wipe us out and take over."

Hard evidence, that's what she wanted, the kind she gathered when she did a biology experiment. It was what she loved about science—all the absolute facts. It was reassuring to have proof that there was some order to the universe, some rules that were always followed.

After what happened today, she didn't know what the rules were anymore. And that frightened her.

"You remember the end of *ET*?" Maria asked suddenly. "How those government guys were going to come in and take him away?"

Liz nodded, her thoughts still on a world where the periodic chart no longer applied.

"Do you think that's what would happen to Max if we told people the truth about him?" Maria continued.

"I don't know," Liz admitted. "I doubt everyone would just be like, Oh, an alien, that's interesting. There must be people out there who would want to study him or do tests on him. They could lock Max away for the rest of his life or even—"

Liz couldn't say it.

"Or even kill him," Maria finished for her.

Liz flashed on an image of Max lying on the ground, still and cold. She felt a rush of pure emotion that went beyond any facts. She couldn't let that happen. She couldn't let Max die.

"We can never tell anyone the truth," she told Maria.

"Never," Maria repeated. "Wait. What about Alex? Can't we even tell him?"

"Maria, no! We can't tell anyone."

Liz wished they could tell Alex. She totally trusted him, and they both told him practically everything. But Max's secret was like a deadly virus—it had to be contained, or someone could die. Max could die.

Maria flicked a crumb off the table. "So, um, what do you think Max *really* looks like?"

"What do you mean?"

"I mean, what are the chances that the *beings* on the planet he came from look exactly like humans? Don't you think the way Max looks must be sort of a disguise?"

Liz didn't know how to answer. Max was just *Max*. She wasn't used to thinking of him as some kind of creature.

Maria stood up and wandered back to the sink. She set the teapot on the stove. "I wonder if he can eat the same food we do. I saw this movie where the aliens could only eat decomposed flesh—you know, where bacteria and bugs did part of the digesting for them."

Liz watched Maria pour tea leaves into little silver balls. She couldn't believe the way her friend was talking about Max. They had both known him forever, but Maria was talking about him as if he were something on the Discovery Channel.

"Maybe he's like the Fly. Maybe he just spews some kind of acid on his food and then—sluurp, sucks it up. What do you think? You're the science guru."

"God, Maria," Liz muttered.

Maria didn't hear her. She kept on chattering away.

43

"Do you think he sees humans as some kind of inferior life-form? Like, are we just lumps of meat to him?"

Max always picked Maria to be on his team when they played softball in the sixth grade—he picked her first, even though she was one of the worst players. He made Paula Perry stop harassing Maria the first year of junior high. He didn't tell his insurance company when Maria dinged his car in the school parking lot last year.

It's like she's forgotten all the nice things he's done for her—and for half the other people in school, Liz thought. Now he's just the alien boy.

No wonder it was so hard for Max to tell Liz the truth about himself. He probably thought she was going to treat him like some kind of freak.

And I did, Liz realized. I practically *ran* out of his room.

She shivered as she pictured Max's eyes. The pain and humiliation filling his beautiful blue eyes as she backed away from him.

I never even thanked him for saving my life.

Come on, Max, Michael thought. Get me out of here.

Right on cue he heard the horn of Max's Jeep. Yes! He couldn't stand being in this house one more second. Michael strode toward the front door, shrugging on his jacket as he walked.

"Hold it," Mr. Hughes called as Michael started past the kitchen. "The backyard looks like a jungle. I want it mowed before you go anywhere."

"It's going to be dark in half an hour," Michael protested.

Mr. Hughes smirked at him. Michael hated that little smirk. "Then you'll have to work fast, won't you?"

Michael didn't want to get into a shouting match with the guy. It wasn't worth it. He struggled to keep his voice calm. "Is there some reason you couldn't have told me you wanted the lawn mowed this morning, or this afternoon, or even an hour ago? Max is outside waiting for me."

"Well, he'll just have to keep waiting. Come and get me when you're finished. I want to see what kind of job you did before you take off anywhere."

Michael hated the way Mr. Hughes was always

playing his little power games. Hughes didn't care about the backyard. That old green truck of his had been up on blocks in the far corner since before Michael moved in. It had totally destroyed that patch of grass, but he didn't care. Hughes only cared about showing Michael who was in charge.

In less than a year I'll be eighteen, Michael thought. Then I'm out of here. No more foster homes. No more foster parents. No more being told that an endless string of strangers are my family.

"Fine. I'll mow the backyard," Michael muttered. Then he walked out the front door and closed it quietly behind him. He trotted over to Max's Jeep to tell him he had to wait.

But when he reached the Jeep, he snapped. Forget Hughes. Forget the idiotic social services people who thought sticking him in strangers' houses meant he was being taken care of. He just couldn't deal with it tonight. He couldn't stand out in the backyard while Hughes inspected his work, finding a dozen little things Michael forgot to do or did wrong.

He climbed into the Jeep. "Floor it," Michael ordered.

Max didn't ask any questions. He just took off down the street, past the well-tended houses and neatly kept yards of the south side.

Michael had lived in every neighborhood in town— from the run-down section by the old military base to the historic district with its big houses and big trees. Living in the historic district was cool. He didn't really care about the nice houses, but he liked living so close to Max and Isabel.

"Where to?" Max asked as they headed out of town, miles and miles of flat desert stretching in front of them.

"I want to try that arroyo we saw on our way back last week." Michael pulled a battered map out of his pocket. He popped open the glove compartment, grabbed a pencil, and began shading in the area he planned to search tonight. It was about sixty miles out of Roswell and fifteen miles from the crash site.

Max glanced over at him. "A couple more years of this, and you'll have half of New Mexico colored in."

"Not quite," Michael answered. They *had* covered a lot of ground over the years. But Michael wanted to do more. He wished he could search all day every day instead of once a week.

"It's been a while since we've found anything. Maybe we're getting too far away from the crash site," Max said.

"We might be too far to find debris, but I still think the ship is stashed somewhere in the desert, not more than a few hours' drive from the site," Michael answered. "They wouldn't want to risk taking it farther. Too many people would have to be involved. There would be too many questions."

Max gave a noncommittal grunt. Michael knew that Max doubted they would ever find the ship. And Isabel kept saying they were fools to keep looking. She'd given up the search a long time ago. But Michael was never going to give up. And Max would keep coming out to the desert with him every week as long as Michael wanted him to. Michael

47

could count on Max. Always could, always would.

Michael clicked on the radio. He didn't really feel like talking, and it didn't seem as if Max did, either. He was probably thinking about Liz.

Michael didn't know what that girl had said to Max when they were alone in his room. But whatever it was, it had totally annihilated him. After she left, Max told Michael and Isabel that Liz would keep their secret. He promised them they weren't in any danger. But Max hadn't sounded happy or even relieved, and he looked like he'd been punched in the gut.

Liz couldn't handle the truth. Michael was sure of that. She probably treated Max like some kind of freak.

We just don't belong, he thought. We're never going to fit in. It's never going to feel right living here. And that's why he had to find a way out. He would make it back to his home planet, his real home, no matter what it took. Maybe he even had some relatives there.

Michael watched the sun sink lower and lower, turning the sky pink and orange. Slowly the colors faded, then turned to black, and stars began to appear.

He wished it could be night all the time. At night somehow it felt like his home planet was closer, almost in reach, up there behind the stars somewhere. At night he felt positive that he would find the ship, positive that he would somehow find his way back.

During the day . . . sometimes during the day it seemed hopeless. It felt like there was nothing up there at all. No home to go back to.

"We're coming up to the arroyo," Max said. "Do you want to drive or hike?"

"Hike." Michael needed to cool off. He figured after a long hike he might be ready to go back and see Mr. Hughes without wanting to punch his face in.

Max parked the Jeep. Michael sprang out and half slid, half climbed down the side of the arroyo. He could hear Max right behind him.

When Michael reached the bottom, he turned in a slow circle, scanning the walls and floor of the arroyo. He didn't know what he was looking for exactly, just something that didn't belong.

One of the other things Michael liked about night was how clearly he could see. His vision was better in the dark than it was during the day. It made the weekly nighttime searches easier. Having the advantage over any curious humans who happened by was a bonus, too.

"I'll go south, you go north?" Max asked.

Michael nodded and set off. We're due to find something, he thought. It's been way too long. It had been almost a year since Max found the strip of thin, flexible metal that they both figured was part of their parents' ship. It had to be. It was like nothing they'd ever seen before. If you crumpled it up, it immediately straightened itself out. It was indestructible. Michael had tried cutting it with pruning shears. He'd even taken a blowtorch to it once. But the metal, if that's what it was, always returned to its original shape, undamaged.

The sound of a bunch of sheep baaing interrupted Michael's thoughts. He stood still and listened. Was someone out there? Someone who had spooked the sheep?

The sheep quieted down again. Now all Michael

could hear was the sound of his own breathing and the tiny scratch, scratch, scratch of a blue belly lizard's claws as it darted across a rock. Guess it was nothing, he decided.

He pulled a plastic bottle out of his backpack and took a swig of the grape soda laced with hot sauce. He knew it would make humans gag, but he figured his taste buds worked differently because he could drink it all day. He hiked forward.

When he was a kid, every time they came out to the desert, he'd been positive they would find the ship. He thought he would just hop in and fly himself and Michael and Isabel home. He was sure that somehow he'd just know exactly how all the controls worked.

Then when he was a couple of years older, he saw that old Superman movie on TV. There was a scene where Superman found a crystal that showed a hologram of his dead father, and he got to have all these conversations with him.

For a long time Michael hoped he'd find something like that crystal. Something that would show him his father's face, at least.

But he grew up. And he never found anything to tell him who he really was. Now all Michael wanted was a clue, a hint. Anything that would lead him to the next place to look. Anything to keep him hoping.

He walked on and on, studying every rock, every crevice. He hadn't even found a gum wrapper when he heard Max's shrill whistle, the signal that it was time to head back.

Max was already in the driver's seat when Michael

climbed back up to the top of the arroyo. Michael didn't ask him if he'd found anything. He already knew the answer.

"Drop me off at the cave on the way back, okay?" Michael asked as he swung into the Jeep. "I think I'm going to sack out there."

Max nodded and turned the Jeep toward town. The cave was about twenty miles outside Roswell, much closer to town than to the crash site.

Michael had spent more time in the cave than he had in any of his foster homes. It was a special place—the first place he had seen when he broke free of his incubation pod. He'd been about seven years old—at least he looked about the same as a seven-year-old human child, although he must have been incubating for about forty years.

He'd wanted to stay in the cave forever. The desert outside seemed too big and bright to him. He felt safer in the dim light with the solid limestone walls all around him.

Michael had spent days huddled next to the un-opened pod—it was the one Max and Isabel shared, but he didn't know that then—pressing himself against its warm surface. The tiny rustling sounds he heard inside it kept him company.

Finally thirst and hunger drove him into the desert. A local rancher found him drinking from the same stream the guy's sheep used. The man took him into town, and Michael was placed in the orphanage. From there he went to his very first foster home.

It took him only a week to learn English. Less

than that for math. The social services people had figured he was at a fifth-grade level when they started
him at Roswell Elementary. They never could figure
out why he didn't remember his parents or where he
came from.

Michael still remembered the day Max brought in
a piece of amethyst to show the class. He had said he
liked it because it was the same color as the ring of
light around their teacher, Mr. Tollifson. All the other
kids laughed. Mr. Tollifson said it was nice that Max
had such a good imagination.

And Michael had the amazing, joy-inducing real-
ization that he wasn't alone anymore. Someone else
could see what he saw.

"Mr. Cuddihy isn't going to be happy if the Hugheses
complain that you've been staying out all night
again," Max commented as they drove down the
empty highway.

"Mr. Cuddihy is never happy," Michael answered.
His social worker would have to deal. And if the
Hugheses made too big a stink about it, Mr. Cuddihy
would probably have to start looking for foster home
number eleven. His social worker would just have to
deal with that, too.

"You can come home with me," Max volunteered.
"My parents won't care."

"Nah. I feel like being by myself," Michael answered.

He wouldn't mind hanging out all night at the
Evanses'. But he didn't want to be there for breakfast
in the morning. Mrs. Evans was always so cheerful.
She'd be asking a million questions about school and

stuff. And Mr. Evans would be reading the comics out loud with all his goofy voices. It was way too much family for Michael to handle.

Sometimes Michael wondered what his life would have been like if the Evanses had been the ones to find him instead of that rancher. If he had just been in a different place at a different time, he could have had Max and Isabel's life, growing up with parents who loved him. Don't even go there, Michael thought. It's pointless.

"You sure you don't want to come back with me?" Max asked. "My mom would probably make you blueberry pancakes, and we have that brown mustard you like to go with them."

Michael shook his head. He was used to being alone now. He was good at it. There was no point in getting used to something that would just get taken away.

Isabel pulled open the top drawer of her dresser and stared inside. Her makeup was neatly organized by use, brand, and color. Maybe I should make little combinations of blush, eye shadow, lipstick, and nail polish, she thought. Then I could just pull out the set that matched whatever outfit I have on and—

No. That would be way too anal. Isabel gently closed the drawer.

She had to stop driving herself nuts over this whole Liz Ortecho situation. If she didn't watch herself, she'd move on to organizing her shoes by heel height and width and embroidering the days of the week on her panties.

Okay, here's what I'll do, Isabel decided. If I get even a hint that Liz is going to open her fat mouth, I'll go into her dreams and find a way to drive her crazy. She can spend the rest of her life in an insane asylum, babbling about aliens. No one will pay any attention to her.

Isabel stretched out on her bed and smiled. Poor Liz. I can see her now. She might even have to get shock treatment.

Now that she had that little problem solved, it was time to decide something really important. What to wear to the homecoming dance. Isabel planned to be crowned homecoming queen, and she wanted to look good. Well, she always looked good. But she wanted to look *good*.

Isabel grabbed a magazine off her night table and started flipping through it. Definitely not that pink froufrou thing, she thought. The girl looks like she went shopping after an overdose of Prozac. Being that happy just wasn't attractive.

And not that red rag with the built-in push-up bra. No, no, no. "Somebody call 1-800-Go Ricki," she mumbled. "I have a candidate for the 'My Best Friend Went to the Homecoming Dance Dressed Like A Hoochie Mama' show."

She threw the magazine on the floor and picked up a movie magazine. She studied a photo of a British movie star going into some premiere wearing an ice blue slip dress. Simple. Sexy. And oh, so Isabel.

She would go shopping tomorrow. All she had to do was talk her dad out of his credit card. It had been a few months since the last time. And the homecoming dance *was* a very important event in a girl's life. He would understand that.

Isabel checked the clock—2 A.M. She'd already gotten in the two hours of sleep she needed, and there were hours and hours to go before she had to get ready for school. She reached for the remote, then changed her mind. Late-night TV sucked. She'd already seen every infomercial about a hundred times. If only humans didn't need so much sleep, there would be good stuff on all night.

She could go see what Max was doing or call up Michael. But they would probably end up arguing about Liz, and Isabel wasn't in the mood.

Isabel checked the clock again. All the guys in Roswell should be asleep by now. She could do some dream walking and make extra sure she would get the votes she needed to be elected homecoming queen. Not that there was any real doubt, but Isabel *was* a junior, and usually the homecoming queen was a senior. Besides, it was something to do.

She closed her eyes and allowed her breathing to become slow and even. Years of practice made it easy for her to slip into the state between sleep and wakefulness, the place where the shimmering dream orbs were visible.

She never got tired of watching the dream orbs swirl around her, like giant soap bubbles blown with an enchanted bubble wand. Each orb gave off one pure note of music, and Isabel had spent a lot of hours matching up the people she knew with the sound of their dream orb.

Who should I choose tonight? Hmmm. I think it's Alex Manes's turn, she decided. She listened for the sonorous sound of Alex's dream orb, a sound so rich, she could almost taste it. Yes, there it was.

Isabel stretched out her arms and began to hum, calling the orb to her. It spun into her hands and she peered into it, feeling like a gypsy with a crystal ball. Inside the orb she could see a miniature version of one of the halls of Ulysses F. Olsen High. Alex was dreaming about school. How fun.

She hummed louder, and the orb expanded. When it was large enough, she stepped through, the surface of the soap bubble soft against her skin.

Alex must have a good visual memory, she thought. His dream version of school was pretty accurate. She giggled as he ran down the hall past her.

"The calculus final can't be today," Alex cried. "It's only October. I didn't study."

"The final isn't today," Isabel said calmly.

Alex spun around to face her. His red hair was mussed, as if he'd been nervously running his fingers through it. "Are you sure? I just saw Mr. O'Brien, and he said the test had already started. He said he was taking off ten points for every second I was late."

"He was teasing you. The only thing you're late for is the homecoming dance." Isabel took Alex by the hand and led him toward the gym. He didn't ask one question. She loved how easy it was to convince people of stuff in dreams.

Isabel pushed open the gym's big double doors. A

spotlight hit her and Alex, and crowns appeared on their heads.

"Can you believe we won?" Isabel asked. "We got elected homecoming queen and king! I think we're supposed to lead this dance."

"Oh. Really? You and me?" Alex blinked into the spotlight.

"You and me." Isabel wrapped her arms around Alex's neck and rested her head on his shoulder. Nice, she thought. Exactly the right height. And he smells good, too.

Isabel usually liked a few more muscles. Washboard abs and powerful legs. But Alex's lean body felt . . . mmmm.

You're here to work, not to have fun, she reminded herself. She raised her head and gazed up at him—the universal language for "kiss me."

Alex's gaze drifted to her lips. He pulled her closer. She could feel his warm breath against her cheeks, then . . .

She snapped herself out of the orb. Her lips curved into a satisfied smile. That's another vote for me, she thought. She loved playing with their minds.

"Smell this." Maria thrust a tiny vial of liquid under Liz's nose. "It's cedar. It's really soothing. You'll go into bio feeling at peace."

Liz obediently took a sniff, but she didn't think anything would make her feel less nervous about seeing Max. How was she going to face him after the way she bolted out of his house? What was she going to say to him?

"Feel better?" Maria asked.

"A little, I guess," Liz fibbed. If she said no, Maria would just make her smell something else. Maria was totally into aromatherapy, and she definitely wanted to convert Liz.

"Now that I know the truth about Max, I—" Liz stopped abruptly as Alex plopped down on the ground next to them with two slices of pizza, a brownie, a bag of fried pork rinds, and an orange soda balanced in his hands.

Alex glanced from Liz to Maria, then back to Liz. "Okay, what's going on? You two look guilty."

"Uh, uh, we were just—," Maria began.

"We were just saying how much we love that new box of tampons—the one where they put all the sizes together," Liz jumped in. Maria was such an awful liar. "They have the junior ones, for really light days, and—"

"Wait," Alex exclaimed. "I'm starting to feel really left out. If you don't stop, I'm going to get my feelings hurt."

"Just admit it," Liz answered. "You can't even take hearing the word *tam*—"

"Okay, okay. You're right," Alex said quickly. "If either of you ever want to break up with a guy but don't know how, just start talking about . . . *that* a lot."

"Sounds like the beginning of one of your lists," Liz said.

"Hey, yeah! I've been trying to figure out what the next one should be," he answered.

Alex had a web site filled with lists like "How to Know When to Bring a Barf Bag to a Movie" and "How to Guarantee Your Kid Will Grow Up to Be a Serial Killer or a Game Show Host." Once he got an idea for a list, he could talk about it for hours. And today that's exactly what Liz wanted him to do. She didn't want to get anywhere near the Max subject, not with Maria, the world's worst liar, sitting next to her.

"Okay, what else, what else?" Alex took a big bite of his pizza.

Maria rummaged around in her purse and pulled out a capsule filled with something green. She handed it to Alex. "Here. If you're going to eat that garbage, you need a little herbal boost. I blended this myself. It has great stuff in it."

Alex squinted at the capsule, then tossed it into his

mouth and washed it down with a big swallow of the orange soda. "Okay, I got it. Here's another great way to get rid of a guy. Tell him you think it would be so cute if you started wearing matching outfits to school."

Liz took a little bite of her sandwich, then set it down. She was too anxious to eat.

"What about Rick Surmacz and Maggie McMahon?" Maria asked. "Maggie makes him wear the same colors as her practically every day, and they've been together since the seventh grade."

"Yeah, but everyone knows Maggie gave Rick a lobotomy," Alex shot back. "He has all the signs. Right, Liz?"

"Huh? Oh yeah," she mumbled. She had kind of stopped paying attention once she was sure Alex was on a safe topic.

"Is something—," Alex began. Then his expression turned grim. "Kyle Valenti at four o'clock."

Oh, great, Liz thought. This is exactly what I need right now.

Kyle plopped down next to her on the grass—without waiting for an invitation. "So, Liz, when are we going out again?" he asked.

He's like a deranged Energizer Bunny, Liz thought. How many times am I going to have to tell him no before his batteries run out?

"That would be *never*. I told you that, Kyle," Liz said firmly. She reached across Maria and grabbed one of Alex's pork rinds. She didn't want one—she thought they were pretty disgusting, actually—but she hoped maybe if she ignored Kyle, he'd just go away.

"Am I missing something? Are you, like, the hottest girl in school? What makes you think you're so special?" Kyle demanded.

Maria nudged Liz. She's probably madder than I am, Liz thought.

"Kyle, get a clue, get some therapy, get a life," Liz said. "Just get over it."

Maria nudged Liz again. "Your shirt," she whispered.

Liz glanced down and saw that her baby tee had ridden up—revealing one of the silver handprints on her stomach. When I reached for the pork rind, she thought.

Did Kyle notice? Probably not, she decided. The prints had begun to fade, and Kyle was pretty distracted by the sound of his own voice. Liz slid the shirt back down, trying to make the movement look casual.

"You should get rid of your attitude," Kyle was saying. "You—"

"That's it, Valenti," Alex interrupted. "Get lost."

Kyle pushed himself to his feet and stared down at Alex. "What—are you going to make me?" Kyle demanded.

Alex stood up and faced off with him. Alex was shorter than Kyle, and he probably weighed twenty-five pounds less. But he didn't back down. He took a step closer.

Wonderful, Liz thought, rolling her eyes. Now I have to be nice to Kyle so that he doesn't kill Alex.

"Look, Kyle," she said in her sweetest voice. "I didn't mean to—"

"Forget it, okay? Don't even bother." Kyle moved

away from Alex and glanced around the quad. He jerked his chin toward Isabel Evans. "Who cares about you? If *she* didn't want to go out with me, then I'd have to be upset." He stalked off.

Alex sat back down. "What a total and complete jerk."

"Yeah, Liz is much, much prettier than Isabel," Maria added.

Liz cracked up. "I don't think that's what he meant," she told Maria.

Maria turned to Alex. "Oh, come on. Liz is way more gorgeous than Isabel, right?"

"Different types," Alex muttered.

"Yeah. Liz treats guys like human beings. Isabel treats guys like dirt," Maria answered. "I don't know why any guy would want to go out with her."

Alex looked over at Isabel. "Yeah. Blond hair, blue eyes, curvy body. Who would want to get close to that?"

Maria whacked him on the shoulder. "I will never understand guys. Just because you like how she looks, you don't care that she has the personality of a taxidermist."

"I had a dream about her the other night, and it had nothing to do with dead animals," Alex protested.

"It's hard to believe she and Max are brother and sister," Liz said. "I mean, yeah, they have the same hair and eyes."

"But not the same curvy body," Alex joked.

Liz ignored him. "But Max's personality is totally different. Max is nice to *everyone*."

Maria grabbed Liz by the arm. "I just realized.

Isabel is Max's sister. Does that mean she's also a—"

Liz slapped her hand over Maria's mouth. She couldn't believe Maria had almost blurted out Max's secret. She was going to have to sit her down and remind her how serious it would be for Max if the truth about him got out.

"A what?" Alex asked.

"Oh no," Liz said. "Don't try to weasel out of it. You have to tell us your dream. You brought it up— that means you have to tell."

Maria pulled Liz's hand off her mouth. She gave Liz a little nod to show she understood. "Yeah. I'll analyze it for you. I've read every dream book there is."

"There's not much to analyze," Alex said.

Another save by Liz Ortecho, Liz thought. She glanced over at Isabel Evans. She looked so, well, normal. But Maria had a good point. *Could* Isabel be an alien, too? She must be—she was Max's sister. Liz knew they were both adopted, and they looked practically like twins. Liz stared around the quad. Were Max and Isabel the only two aliens at school? Or were there aliens everywhere, and she just hadn't known about it?

"Come on," Maria said. "Details, Alex."

"Okay, but try not to laugh." Alex looked embarrassed. "I was at the homecoming dance with Isabel— and we were the homecoming king and queen. We had on the crowns and everything."

"Oh, stop. I'm going to hurl." Maria made loud barfing sounds.

"What do you think? Is it a sign? Should I try and

get up the guts to, like, talk to her or something?" Alex asked.

"No!" Liz blurted.

Alex looked hurt.

But Liz couldn't worry about his feelings. She'd suddenly remembered something about Isabel. The other day, at Max's house, Isabel had stared at Liz with pure hatred.

She's afraid I'm going to betray Max, Liz realized. And if people discovered Max was an alien, they'd know Isabel was one, too. Liz's stomach began to tingle. Isabel must be terrified. No wonder she hated Liz. Would she come after me? Liz wondered. Try to hurt my friends?

Liz didn't know. But she did know one thing—she didn't want Alex anywhere near Isabel.

"It's just that, like Maria said, she treats guys like dirt," Liz told Alex. "You deserve better."

"I guess you're right," Alex said. But Liz noticed he was staring at Isabel when he said it.

"I have this craving for a doughnut. Want to go to the doughnut place?" Max asked. He ate the last bite of his burger and shoved the tray across the cafeteria table.

"But that would mean . . . cutting school." Michael opened his gray eyes wide and stared at Max with mock horror.

Max sniffed the air. "Can you smell them? Can you smell the crullers sliding out of the oven?" He pulled a couple of packets of hot sauce out of his jacket pocket and waved them in front of his friend's face. He knew crullers with hot sauce were Michael's favorite.

"I have a history test, and I would not think of jeopardizing my education for a cruller," Michael said primly.

"Have you ever had one when they're still hot, because I think today is cruller baking day," Max said.

"Do you think I'm that easy?" Michael demanded. "Besides, it's not like you can hide from the girl for the rest of your life."

"Yeah, you're right." Max didn't bother to pretend that he didn't know who Michael was talking about.

The bell rang. "I kind of like giving you advice for a change," Michael said as they headed out.

"Don't get too used to it," Max answered. He started up the stairs to his advanced placement bio class. Would Liz even be there? He'd thought about bailing—why wouldn't she?

Max couldn't decide if he hoped she'd be there or not. He wanted to see her and make sure she was okay. But he couldn't take it if she looked at him the way she did on Saturday, all scared and weirded out and . . . and *repulsed*. Man, he would never forget the expression on her face.

He hesitated outside the door. Don't be a wuss, he told himself, and stepped inside. Liz was there. He should have known she wouldn't cut. She wasn't really the kind of person who backed away from things.

He knew she noticed him come in—her shoulders tensed a little, and the sickly yellow steaks that still marred her amber aura grew a little darker. But she didn't look up. She kept her eyes focused on the lab table as she set up their microscope.

Max took a detour to check on the lab mice. Admit it, he thought as he fed them a few pieces of celery. You're stalling. "Wish me luck," he whispered to Fred, his favorite mouse. Then he forced himself to walk over to the lab station he shared with Liz.

"We're doing a comparison between animal and plant cells today," Liz said in a rush when Max slid onto his lab stool. "I'm trying to decide which category a couch potato would fall into."

Her laugh sounded a little fake. But at least she was trying to joke around with him the way she usually did—even if she still hadn't managed to look at him.

If Liz was going to act as if nothing had happened, he would, too. We should both get Oscar nominations after this class, Max thought.

"Okay, let's get started," Ms. Hardy called. "Everyone on the left, use a vegetable scraping to make a slide. Everyone on the right, use a swab to get some cells from the inside of your cheek and do a slide. When you've answered the questions on your own slide—animal or plant—then trade with another team and answer the rest."

Max picked up one of the swabs. "I'll do it."

Liz grabbed the swab away. "Are you crazy?" she demanded. She lowered her voice. "Do you even know what your cells look like? What if they don't look . . . the same?"

She was right. Ms. Hardy often walked around and looked at their slides. And if there was something *different* about his cells, she would definitely notice.

Max was usually so careful, so cautious. He couldn't believe he'd almost done something that amazingly stupid. This thing with Liz had him totally messed up. All he could think about was her. He couldn't stop wondering what was going on in her head.

Liz wiped the inside of her mouth with the swab. Max pulled a chipped glass slide out of the little wooden box and handed it to her. She ran the swab over the glass, then Max dropped a thin plastic slide cover on top of the cell sample she'd deposited.

At least we can still do this, he thought. They had always been a perfect match as lab partners.

"I wanted to talk to you about what happened on Saturday," Liz said. She slipped the side under the microscope's metal clips, then peered into the eyepiece, checking the focus.

Yeah, Liz definitely doesn't back away from things, Max thought. Pretending nothing had happened might have been easier, but it just wasn't her.

"Telling me the truth must have been so hard, and then I totally flipped out on you," Liz continued. "I didn't even thank you for saving my life." She used the knob on the side of the microscope to make a few minor adjustments, then looked up at Max. Her gaze was direct and steady, but Max saw a tiny muscle in her eyelid jump.

It's taking everything she has to do this, he thought. She can't even look at me anymore without it being this huge effort.

"I don't know what to say. 'I'm sorry' sounds so lame.

But I'm really sorry," she told him. "And thanks . . . thanks for saving my life."

"You're welcome." Max turned away and checked the lab book. "We're supposed to do a sketch and label the organelles." He pulled out a sheet of paper and pushed it toward Liz. "You'd better do the drawing. We both know I can't even draw stick figures."

Liz looked into the eyepiece again. She picked up a pencil and drew a big circle, still studying the slide.

"Start with the Golgi apparatus," Max suggested. "Do you see it? It's supposed to look like a stack of deflated balloons."

Liz shifted position, and a lock of her dark hair tumbled over her shoulder and fell across the drawing. Max started to brush it back—and she jerked away.

She bent down and fiddled with her shoe. "I . . . I tripped," she stammered. "The heel on this shoe always wobbles. I keep forgetting to take it to the shoe repair." The yellow streaks in her aura widened until they almost blotted out the amber.

Max knew she was lying. She didn't stumble. She jerked away from him because she couldn't stand for him to touch even a strand of her hair.

We can both try to act normal, Max thought. We can both say the right things. But it's never going to be the same between us again. Liz is afraid of me.

"So what kind of mood is *el jefe* in today?" Liz asked Stan, the cook on duty at the Crashdown Cafe.

Stan grabbed a spatula in each hand and flipped two burgers in perfect unison. "The boss man has been listening to the Dead all day," he answered.

"Cool." Liz and everyone else at the Crashdown could tell how Mr. Ortecho was feeling by what kind of CDs he played. You couldn't get better than the Grateful Dead on her father's musical mood scale.

Liz hurried into his office. She couldn't help smiling at the sight of her papa's compact beer belly pushing against his tie-dyed T-shirt.

"I think for your birthday I'm going to have to replace that shirt with a bigger one. You know, eating Cherry Garcia ice cream isn't the only way of expressing your love for Jerry," she teased.

"Not the only, just the best," Papa answered. "And don't even think about replacing this shirt. I bought it at the concert where you were conceived. Uncle John's Band was—"

Liz slapped her hands over her ears. "I don't want to hear any more, thank you." She did not need the details of her parents' sex life.

Her father laughed. "What are you doing here, anyway? You're not working today."

Liz lowered her hands. "I have to talk to you about something important."

His expression turned serious. "Is it something with school?"

"No, it's nothing with school." Liz sighed. "Why do you always think it's something with school? It's never anything about school, all right?"

Sometimes Liz felt like throwing back her head and screaming, "I am not Rosa." Because that's what this whole thing was about. It was about Rosa. She'd been dead almost five years, but in so many ways she was still the most important member of Liz's family. She was there in the things they said to one another and in the things they never said.

Liz knew exactly why her father was always on her case about school. The year before Rosa died, her grades started slipping. Liz's parents got Rosa a tutor and stuff, but they didn't realize that the grades were only a tiny part of the trouble Rosa was in.

Liz glanced over at Papa. He stared down at some invoices on his desk, but his eyes were blank. Liz knew that expression so well. He was doing it again. Wondering what if. What if he had paid more attention. What if he had put Rosa in private school. What if he'd read more about teenagers and drugs. What if, what if, what if.

"I'm pretty sure I'm going to be valedictorian," Liz said, trying to pull her papa out of his dark thoughts. "You'd better start thinking about what to wear to my graduation because everyone is going to be looking at you and Mama, parents of the girl making the brilliant speech."

"Make sure you mention the cafe," Papa said. He shoved the papers away and looked up at Liz. "If it's not about school, what is this something important?"

"It's our uniforms. The seventies *Star Trek* rip-offs we wear have a certain kind of cool retro thing going, but Maria and I would really like to move into the future." Liz held up a photo of Tommy Lee Jones and Will Smith in their *Men in Black* suits and shades. "We were thinking something like this."

Mr. Ortecho shook his head. "You want me to spend money on new uniforms when there is absolutely nothing wrong with the old ones? That's not good business, Liz."

Liz pouted for a second. Then she went in for the kill. "Oh, well. The guys do seem to like looking at us in those short skirts. Our tips would probably go down if we switched to the suits."

"Wait, who is looking?" Papa demanded. "Who, exactly?"

Mrs. Ortecho opened the office door and inched her way in, a huge baking sheet balanced in her hands. Flour dotted her baggy overalls and her short brown hair. "I just brought over my latest creation, and I had to show it off," she told them.

Ignoring her papa's frown, Liz grabbed one side of the baking sheet and helped her mother lower it to the desk. She gave a snort of laughter as she studied the cake. "An alien riding a horse?"

Mrs. Ortecho shrugged. "It's for Benji Sanderson's birthday. He loves cowboys, and this *is* Roswell."

"At least you didn't have to do another spaceship," Mr. Ortecho said.

Liz's mama loved coming up with new designs for her cakes and wanted challenges from her customers. But she kept getting orders for spaceships and aliens, aliens and spaceships.

Mrs. Ortecho had to settle for creating her own masterpieces for the birthdays of each of Liz's billion relatives. She'd made an amazing 3-D cake portrait of Abuelita's favorite dog, and everyone had been blown away by the Dracula cake she came up with for cousin Nina's eighth birthday. She molded a coffin out of chocolate and put a strawberry-jam-filled vampire cake inside.

Stan popped his head into the office. "Liz, you're not going to believe who is out front to see you—Elsevan DuPris."

Liz's heart jumped to her throat, but she tried to keep calm in front of her parents.

This was not good. Elsevan DuPris published the *Astral Projector,* Roswell's answer to the *National Enquirer.* Every story in the *Projector* had something to do with aliens. It was a pretty big coincidence that DuPris wanted to talk to Liz two days after she got absolute proof that aliens exist. A big, scary coincidence.

"You coming?" Stan asked.

"Yeah. I'm interviewing DuPris for a paper I'm writing," she lied to her parents. Then she slipped past Stan and headed for the front of the cafe.

"Get me some costs on those new uniforms," Mr. Ortecho called after her.

It was easy to spot DuPris lounging against the counter. If he's not here to ask me to be his personal shopper, he should be, Liz thought. He was wearing a rumpled white suit with a lime green shirt, a white Panama hat, and white lace-up shoes, and he carried a walking stick with an ivory handle. His blond hair was slicked back with a little too much gel, and his smile was a little too oily.

Liz felt herself relax as she strolled over to him. Anyone who went out of the house looking like that had to be a total buffoon. She could handle DuPris, no problemo. "You wanted to see me?" she asked.

"Yes, if you would be so kind as to spare me a moment. Could we sit?" DuPris started toward a booth in the back without waiting for an answer.

Liz followed him. "What can I do for you?" she asked as she slid into the booth across from him. She figured a friendly, I've-got-nothing-to-hide-here approach was the way to go, at least until she found out what he knew.

"I've been hearing some interesting things about you, young lady," DuPris drawled. He sounded like a Scarlett O'Hara wanna-be.

I could do a better accent, Liz thought. And I'm about as far from a Southern belle as you can get.

"What kind of interesting things?" she asked. She made sure to look DuPris straight in the eye. She wondered if he wore colored contacts. His eyes were almost as green as his shirt.

73

"I heard that you almost died a couple of nights ago. I heard you got shot—and that a young man healed the wound simply by touching it," DuPris said.

He got the straight dope, Liz thought. Those two tourists must have blabbed. She decided she needed to get a little creative.

"It probably looked like that guy healed me. But that's not what happened." Liz leaned across the table and lowered her voice. "See, the uniforms we wear here are made of RosWool. That's wool made from sheep that have grazed on the crash site. People say it has powers, and after what happened to me, I believe it. I'd be dead if I had been wearing polyester when I was shot."

DuPris raised his eyebrows. "RosWool?"

"Yeah. There's a company that will make anything you want out of the stuff. I'm thinking of ordering a ski mask—in case I get shot in the head next time."

DuPris was silent for a moment.

"I like you, Ms. Ortecho," he finally said. "I'm a great admirer of a lively sense of humor. Now would you like to tell me what really happened?"

"I just told you," Liz answered. "I think you should definitely write a story about RosWool for your paper. It's something people should know about. Maybe you could even get them to run an ad or something."

"I'm still intrigued by the young man my sources mentioned." DuPris leaned toward her, and Liz caught a whiff of his pine-scented aftershave. It made the inside of her nose itch.

"There *was* a guy who ran up to me," Liz admitted.

"He might have put his hand over the wound to stop the bleeding. But the wool was already working. That's what healed me."

She widened her eyes and tried to look innocent and stupid. DuPris stared at her for a few seconds, then sighed.

"Well, I thank you for setting the record straight." He stood up. "I must say I'm relieved that the young man wasn't responsible for saving your life."

"What? Why?" Liz knew she shouldn't ask. It would have been smarter to let DuPris walk away. But the questions just popped out of her mouth.

DuPris grinned down at her. "You seem like such an intelligent person," he said. "So tell me, if there were a young man who could heal with a touch, isn't it logical to assume he could also *kill* with a touch?" DuPris asked.

Liz shook her head. "I'm not sure what you mean."

DuPris eased back down into the seat across from her, his green eyes intense. "Let's say a young man could manipulate the muscles and skin and even the internal organs to close a bullet wound with a single touch of his hand."

Liz nodded, afraid to speak.

"Well, if the young man could do that, couldn't he also do it in reverse? Couldn't he *open* a hole in a person's heart or cause a rip to appear in one of their lungs—all with the same touch of his hand?"

Liz could almost see the blood pumping through the hole in the heart and the delicate lung tissue tearing open. She grimaced as the gruesome images filled her mind.

"I wouldn't like to think there was someone wandering around our town who could kill so easily and with so little chance of being stopped," DuPris finished.

Standing up again, he tipped his hat at Liz and sauntered toward the door.

Liz rubbed her finger back and forth over the shiny silver tabletop after he left. What DuPris said *did* make sense. Could Max kill someone just by touching them?

"We should all go shopping together for the homecoming dance." Stacey Scheinin gave a little bounce on her toes.

Stacey was always bouncing, or squealing, or giggling. She was like a cheerleader out of some thirteen-year-old boy's fantasies. She made Isabel want to puke.

"I thought all of you could get dresses in the same color—maybe lavender," Stacey went on. "That way when I get elected homecoming queen, all my attendants will be color coordinated. We are going to look totally killer up on the stage together."

"Is there some reason you think *we* are going to be *your* attendants?" Isabel asked.

"Oh, Izzy, don't worry," Stacey cooed. "You can come over tonight and I'll do a makeover on you. I know I can pretty you up enough to be chosen as part of my homecoming court."

"No thanks." Isabel ran her eyes up and down Stacey. "I've seen your work."

"Go, girl," Tish Okabe murmured.

The cheerleading squad was split between girls

who wanted to be just like Stacey and girls who thought Stacey was the love child of Jerry Springer and Lassie. Isabel and Tish were definitely in the second group.

"Let's get back to work." Stacey clapped. "We're going to do Alien Attack until we get it perfect. Izzy, you were behind last time."

"Yeah, me and everyone else but you," Isabel muttered as she moved into place on the gym floor.

"Ready, okay!" Stacey called.

"Roswell aliens, causing a sensation," Isabel began. She caught a flash of movement out of the corner of her eye. Alex Manes slipped through the gym door. He leaned against the back wall, watching her. Just her.

Isabel did a walkover and slid into a split as the cheer ended. She gave Alex a wink, and a grin stretched across his face. That dream did it, she thought. Alex's vote is in the bag. If anyone needs to buy a lavender attendant's dress, it's Stacey. She pushed herself to her feet, her sneakers squeaking against the polished wood floor.

"Okay, everyone, next practice is Wednesday at three-thirty. Be on time, please," Stacey called.

She needs to get out more, Isabel thought. Being head cheerleader is the best thing that's happened to her in her whole pathetic life.

Isabel started toward the locker room. Alex hurried up before she reached the door.

"Hey," he said. He stuck his hands in his back pockets, took them out, then shoved them back in again.

77

He's nervous. How sweet, Isabel thought. "That's it?" she teased. "Just 'hey'? I thought guys were supposed to have some suave opening lines memorized for situations like this."

"That was it," Alex admitted.

"Catchy." Isabel released her long blond hair from its ponytail and shook it out.

"Thought it up all by myself," he bragged. "But I have a backup. It's total cheese. My older brother taught it to me. Want to hear it?"

"Of course." Isabel ran her tongue over her bottom lip. That got Alex's attention. Guys were so predictable. And they never realized when they were being played.

"Okay, pretend I'm a cop, you know, with a gun and badge and stuff," Alex instructed.

Isabel laughed. "I like this one already. Are you wearing handcuffs, too?"

"No way. I told you this is my brother's line, and he's a classy guy. Okay, get ready to melt." Alex cleared his throat loudly. "I'm going to have to arrest you."

Isabel batted her eyes. "But I haven't done anything wrong."

"Uh, I'm afraid that's not true." A faint blush colored Alex's cheeks. "It's clear you've stolen the stars from the sky—I can see them in your eyes."

Isabel tried not to laugh, but the expression on Alex's face was just too funny. He's not my type, she thought. But he's pretty damn adorable. I wonder if he has freckles everywhere.

"You liked that, huh?" Alex asked.

78

"Yeah," Isabel admitted. She'd never bothered to talk to Alex before, even though they had a bunch of classes together. But there was something about that dream they shared that kept her standing there, smiling at him.

"So, you want to go to the movies or something this weekend, now that I've proved what a suave guy I am?" Alex asked.

"No, but I'll go out with your brother," Isabel shot back. Enough was enough. One *interesting* dream wasn't enough to make her lower her standards.

Alex suddenly appeared completely fascinated by the row of spirit posters behind the bleachers. "Well, my brother did teach it to me," he mumbled. "But I put some of my own refinements on it."

"I've got to hit the showers," Isabel said.

"Um, okay. I'll give your name to my brother." Alex turned around and headed toward the big double doors at the far end of the gym.

Isabel allowed herself a moment to enjoy the rear view, then started for the locker room. Stacey fell in beside her. "New boyfriend, Izzy?"

"Him? No. He's just a pathetic wanna-be," Isabel answered. "I always have a few love slaves following me around with their tongues hanging on the ground. I guess you don't have that problem, huh, Stace?"

Isabel grinned as she strolled into the locker room. Life is good, she thought. In a few days Stacey was going to be *her* attendant at the homecoming dance. And Isabel had just acquired a new little boy toy to play with. There was nothing more fun than a human with a crush.

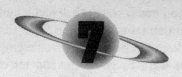

Alex watched Liz and Maria flip through a row of
dresses. He hoped they would hurry it up. The tiny
boutique was making him claustrophobic. The racks
were too close together, and the place smelled like it
had been wallpapered with those little perfume cards
that came in the middle of magazines.

"You're not being much help, Alex. We brought
you along to get a guy's point of view. What kind of
dress would get your attention?" Maria asked.

"Oh, you know, short, tight, backless, low cut, maybe
a couple of slits somewhere," he answered. "Preferably
worn braless with one of those thong things."

Liz whapped him on the head, and Alex grinned.
He loved saying things he knew would pull her chain.
He'd never done the whole girls-as-friends thing before he met Liz and Maria—well, not since he was,
like, seven. It was pretty cool.

And the fact that it bugged the Major was a bonus.
Alex's dad wanted him to spend his time starting up
an ROTC program at school or at least thinking about
what branch of the military he wanted to join after
grad. Ever since his father had retired, he'd become
obsessed with Alex's future military career. The idea

of Alex spending all afternoon playing fashion consultant would make him go ballistic, not that Alex was planning on telling him.

One of the things he wasn't telling was that there was no possible way he was going into the military. He used to hope one of his older brothers would be a trailblazer for him and soften the old man up toward the idea of having a civilian for a son. But his two oldest brothers had joined the air force, just like Dad. And Jesse, his last hope, had just signed up with the marines. The Major wasn't too happy about having a squid in the family, but he had finally switched over from shouting to muttering.

"How about this one?" Liz held up a silky dark blue dress with thin little straps. It looked sort of like a nightgown or something. "That's a definite ten on the man-o-meter," Alex said.

"Whatever this man-o-meter is, don't show it to me," Maria mumbled.

Alex ignored her. He was imagining that silky stuff under his fingers. The material was so thin, he'd be able to feel the warmth of Isabel's skin through the cloth. Isabel. Oh, man. He was doing it again. He had given himself strict orders not to think about Isabel, but she kept popping into his head.

Forget about her, he told himself. Remember what she called you—a pathetic wanna-be. She didn't even bother to wait for you to get all the way out of the gym before she started making fun of you with Stacey.

But there was something about Isabel, something about the way she looked at him while they were talking. . . . There was an attraction between them, a *connection*. Alex couldn't believe she was quite as cold as she seemed. If they could just get away from her little cheerleader clique and all their crap, he had a feeling something could develop between them.

"So are you going to try it on?" Maria asked Liz.

Liz checked the price tag and grimaced. She showed it to Maria. "I think we're in the wrong store."

"Let's try the Clothes Barn," Maria suggested.

Alex led the way out of the store. He took a deep breath of the nonperfumed air. The smells of the mall's food court filled his nose—chocolate cookies mixing with chow mein, tacos, and fries. Much better.

"You know, we've been sort of selfish," Maria said to Liz. "Alex is going to the dance, too. He might need us to help *him* with a little shopping. I'm seeing a collarless shirt and—"

"Don't even think about it," Alex warned them. "I'm not a Just My Size Ken doll."

"Alex, you're seventeen years old. It's time to explore fabrics beyond flannel and denim," Liz put in.

"I wear other stuff. I wear cotton. And . . . what sweatpants are made of—I wear that."

Maria grabbed him by the arm and started dragging him down the walkway. "Macy's is right over there, just waiting for you."

Alex spotted Michael Guerin and Max Evans heading toward them. "Guys!" he yelled in relief. "Hey, guys, you have to help me." He broke away from Maria and hurried over to them. "The makeover mafia has me in their clutches."

"They do look pretty dangerous," Michael said as Liz and Maria joined the group.

"They're trying to use force to make me stop wearing flannel," Alex complained.

He expected Maria to jump in and try to get Max and Michael on her side. But she'd suddenly gotten quiet. Liz, too. What was up with them? They were *never* quiet.

"Don't let them, man," Michael answered. "If they can't accept you as you are, just walk away. Right, Max?"

"Every American has the right to wear flannel," Max answered. He leaned over the railing and stared into the fountain in the lower level. It was obvious he didn't really feel like talking.

Alex didn't know Max that well, but he'd always seemed like a cool guy. Alex wouldn't mind asking him a couple of questions about Isabel, something that would help him figure her out.

Maybe her brother would know which Isabel was real—the Isabel who had flirted with Alex and acted like she was totally enjoying herself? Or the Isabel who had cut him down behind his back?

"What is it with chicks?" Michael asked. "They can have a guy who's crazy about them, but that's not good enough. They have to get in there and start changing things. Guys don't do that. Max, you like Liz just the way she is, right?"

There was a strange little silence.

Liz shot Michael a look that said "back off" loud and clear. Alex frowned. What was going on with everyone? Liz wasn't usually so touchy.

"I mean, you'd never tell her what to wear," Michael amended, avoiding Liz's eyes.

"Liz looks good in everything," Max answered. He pushed himself away from the rail and turned back to face the group. "You even looked cute in that dress you hated, the goofy one with the cupcakes on it."

"You remember that?" Liz cried. "I hated that dress so much, but my *abuelita* gave it to me, so my parents were always making me wear it."

"I don't remember it. What grade was that?" Maria asked.

Liz thought about it a second. "Kindergarten. I remember Ms. Gliden let me wear one of the finger-painting smocks when I had to wear the dress to school. She was so nice. She . . ." Liz's voice trailed off.

Maria was frowning. "But Max wasn't in your kindergarten class, was he?" she asked.

Liz turned to Max. "I have to talk to you alone. Right now." She strode away from the group. Max hesitated a moment, then followed her.

Another strange little silence. Maria had gone pale.

"All righty, then," Alex muttered.

"I have to buy some nail polish," Maria blurted. "I'll meet you at the food court." She rushed toward the escalator.

Alex looked at Michael and shrugged. "You want to get some food?" he asked.

"I can always eat," Michael answered.

Liz and Maria must have popped a few psycho pills when I wasn't looking, Alex thought as he and

Michael headed down the walkway. I hope they wear off fast.

"Don't even think about it," Isabel snarled at the perfume sample guy before he could spray her. She usually avoided this entrance to Macy's. It was like trying to maneuver through a minefield of perfume bombs. The smell of all the scents—flowery, spicy, fruity, powdery—made her stomach turn over.

"Hey, he was kind of a cutie," Tish protested.

Isabel glanced over her shoulder. "He's too bulky and bulgy. Look at those veins popping out on his neck."

"I thought you loved that muscle beach look." Tish held her wrist out to a pale woman in a white smock, who delicately spritzed her with a floral scent.

"I must be maturing. Guys like that seem a little too *obvious* to me now," Isabel said. "Besides, who wants a guy who spends more hours in the gym than he does with you?"

Yeah, that's it, Isabel thought. It didn't have anything to do with the memory of the way Alex's lean body felt pressed up against hers in their dream dance.

"I like it," Tish said. "I still say he's cute."

"You think everyone is cute," Isabel shot back.

"Pretty much everyone has something cute about them, even if it's just one little thing," Tish insisted. "Like that guy by the glove counter. Bad clothes, bad hair, bad skin—"

"Bad personal hygiene," Isabel cut in.

"But look at his mouth." Tish grabbed Isabel's chin

and turned her head toward the guy. "Look at those big, cushy lips. Yum."

"Okay, what about him?" Isabel jerked her head toward a pudgy guy who would probably be calling the Hair Club for Men about a year after grad.

"How can you even ask?" Tish exclaimed. "Look at his butt. Pure Charmin. Don't you just want to squeeze it?"

"Uh, not really," Isabel answered. She scanned the crowd, then smiled. "Okay, I've got a tough one for you—over there by the Lancôme counter."

Tish glanced over and started making gagging noises. "It's the Anticute. Let's get out of here. We see Stacey way too much at school."

"I want to talk to her," Isabel said.

"Is-a-bel." Tish said her name in a long whine.

"Come on." Isabel sauntered toward Stacey. She didn't bother to check and see if Tish was following her. Tish always followed Isabel.

"Hey, Stacey, looking for a lipstick to go with your lavender dress?" Isabel asked.

Stacey whirled toward them.

Tish gasped. "What happened to your face?" she exclaimed.

"I had this horrible dream, and I kept scratching myself in my sleep," Stacey admitted. She ran her fingers over one of the long red scratches covering her face.

I don't think I've ever seen Stacey when she's not bouncing or giggling or something, Isabel thought. Stacey was nauseatingly, unrelentingly bubbly. Even in classes she was constantly doodling little hearts, stars, and rainbows on the cover of her notebook.

86

"That's terrible. Do they hurt?" Tish asked.

Oh, please, Isabel thought. If Tish found a hurt rattlesnake on the sidewalk, she'd probably take it home, nurse it back to health, tie a bow around its neck, and then be surprised when it bit her. She should go out with Max. They'd make a perfect couple.

"They don't really hurt, but they look so gross. I'm trying to find something to cover them up." Stacey studied the foundations and powders in the case in front of her.

"What was your dream about, anyway?" Tish said.

"Oh, it was gross!" Stacey rubbed her face with both hands. "There were all these bugs crawling on me. I could feel all their little legs. I kept scratching and scratching, but I couldn't get them off."

Isabel gave a loud gasp. She opened her eyes wide. "This is *so* weird. I had exactly the same dream last night!"

"What's up?" Max asked as he trotted after Liz.

Liz didn't answer. She turned down a short hallway with a pay phone, a drinking fountain, and one bench. No one would bother them here.

She spun around and glared at Max. "How did you know about my cupcake dress?" she demanded. "Can you read minds? Is that one of your powers? If it is, you have got to find a way to turn it off because it's an incredible invasion of privacy."

Liz didn't even want to think about what Max could have seen in her head. All the embarrassing little things she'd never told anyone, not even Maria.

The silly daydreams she let herself slide into when one of her teachers got so boring, she wanted to scream. The mean little thoughts she had about people sometimes.

But most of all she was afraid that Max had seen all the horrible things she'd thought when he told her he was an alien. Liz was ashamed of the mix of revulsion and fear that flooded her in that moment. If she'd felt those kinds of emotions directed at *her*, she'd be devastated.

"I can't read minds. At least not usually," Max told her. "But when I heal someone, I make a connection with them. I get this rush of images, so fast I can hardly take them all in. And somehow I just *know* things. Not thoughts, exactly. But like that dress—an image of it flashed into my mind, and I knew how you felt about it."

Liz folded her arms over her chest. "What else did you see besides the dress?"

"Um . . . I saw a stuffed dog with a chewed-up ear," Max said.

"Oh, Mr. Beans. He lives on my bed." Liz started to feel a little better. If Mr. Beans and the cupcake dress were the worst things Max saw, that wasn't so bad.

"Liz Ortecho sleeping with a stuffed animal. That's hard to picture." Max laughed. "You're always so intense and focused."

"I don't actually *sleep* with him," Liz corrected. "At night I put him on my dresser."

Max raised his eyebrows. "Oh, really?" he teased.

"Okay, every once in a while, like when I'm sick

or something, I still sleep with him," Liz admitted, blushing. "But you already knew that, didn't you?"

"Lucky guess. You sounded just a little defensive when you said you put him on your dresser," Max explained. "It really bothers you that I got images from your mind, doesn't it?"

Liz looked down at her boots. Even though Max had only seen stupid little things from her childhood, it *did* bother her. What if he were just being polite, telling her the stuff that wasn't important? What if he really had seen everything, like how angry she felt at her sister for dying? He would think she was a horrible person—and she couldn't bear that.

Max wouldn't lie to me, she told herself. If he says he only saw the ugly cupcake dress, then he means it.

"Maybe I overreacted," Liz said slowly. "It's not like you were intentionally spying on me. But, well, how would *you* feel if I knew all your secrets?"

Max stared at her as if she were an idiot. And suddenly Liz felt her face flush. How could she have said that? She *did* know Max's biggest secret, something much more intimate and personal than anything he knew about her.

Max sat down on the little bench. He patted the spot next to him. "Come on, I want to try something."

"O-kaay." Liz wished that hadn't come out sounding so apprehensive. Why couldn't she remember how to act around Max anymore?

She sat next to him. Her shoulder brushed against his. She wanted to move back, but she held herself perfectly still. If she kept jumping away from him,

Max might think she was afraid of him or something.

And I'm not, she thought. Not much.

She wanted to feel completely comfortable around Max, the way she used to. But it was like there was a loop in her head playing the words *he's an alien, he's an alien* over and over.

"I've never tried this before, but I thought maybe I could make the connection go the other way," Max told her. "So that you could invade *my* privacy and get some images from me."

Liz blinked in surprise. What would it be like to see into Max's thoughts? I'd probably be the first human to ever see into the mind of an alien, she thought. The scientist in her was totally excited by the opportunity. But it wouldn't be fair to Max.

"You don't have to do that, Max," Liz said softly. "I was being a jerk about the whole thing. You saved my life—I should be down on my knees thanking you, no matter what your method was."

"No, we have to try this," Max insisted. "Think of it as an experiment. Or as a free movie—the *Max Evans Show.*"

He sounded like a little kid trying to convince his baby-sitter to let him stay up until eleven. He's trying so hard to make me feel okay about what's happened, Liz thought. Why can't I do that for him?

"I have to touch you, okay?" Max asked. "That's how I make the connection."

If he can heal with a touch, can he kill with a touch? The question leaped into Liz's mind. Without thinking, she backed away from Max on the bench.

Instantly his blue eyes grew darker, as if a thick

black curtain had fallen over his emotions.

"Never mind," he said quickly. "It was a stupid idea. Why would you want to be connected to me?"

Max started to stand up, but Liz grabbed his arm. She couldn't let him feel this way, feel as if she were disgusted by him.

"I want to do it. Really," Liz told him.

Max sat back down, smiling. He reached out and tucked her hair behind her ears, then gently cupped her face with his hands. Liz felt a shiver rush through her body. And it didn't feel quite like a frightened shiver.

Max leaned close, so his face was inches from her own. His gaze drifted to her lips, and for one long, shocking moment she thought he was going to kiss her. Instead he began to speak, his voice low and soothing. "Now take deep breaths, and try to let your mind blank out."

Her heart was beating so hard, she could hardly breathe at all. Liz concentrated on pulling in a long, deep breath, then she let it out.

Max matched each of his breaths to hers. She could feel the warm puffs of air on her face each time he exhaled, and the smell of his wintergreen Life Saver filled her nose.

She'd never seen such intense blue as his eyes. It was almost like looking through a deep, deep pool. . . .

Liz realized she was leaning toward him, wanting to be closer, wanting to see *through* those amazing eyes. . . .

She closed her eyes, but she could still feel his eyes on hers. She tried to focus all her attention on her breathing. If thoughts began to intrude, she imagined them drifting away, soundless and weightless.

She heard her heartbeat slow as her relaxation grew deeper and deeper. Slowly she became aware of a second heartbeat. Max's heartbeat. It was like they shared one body now.

An image appeared against the dark screen of her eyelids. A child with bright eyes ripping free of something that looked like a cocoon. Another image quickly replaced the first. A Mr. Wizard junior chemistry set. The images came faster and faster. A sky filled with acid green clouds. A bowl with two turtles sunning themselves. A pair of almond-shaped eyes without whites or irises, just pure black.

Then Liz in the elementary school library, her dark brown braids touching the page of her book. Liz, a little older, swinging at a baseball. Liz standing proudly in front of her ninth-grade science fair project. Liz dressed up for the junior prom. Liz smiling, frowning, giggling, crying. Liz lying on the floor of the cafe. Liz staring at Max with an expression of horror on her face.

Liz opened her eyes and found her gaze locked with Max's. She reached up and slid his hands away from her face. She pressed her fingers together to keep them from trembling.

"Did it work?" he asked. "Did you see anything?"

Liz nodded, not trusting her voice. She'd seen *everything*. She knew everything.

Max was in love with her. He had always been in love with her.

Liz read the question for the third time. "What were the benefits of the gold standard?"

I did study for this test, she thought. I looked at my notes and reread the key parts of the chapters. So why do I have no memory of what the gold standard even is?

Liz skipped down to the multiple-choice section and sighed. *A, B, C,* and *D* all sounded like reasonable choices. But even *E*, none of the above, was a possibility.

Where was her head? Yeah, like I haven't had any distractions lately, she thought. I only almost died. And then found out a guy I've known half my life is an alien. And then found out that this alien guy loves me.

Max Evans loved her. Liz was still trying to wrap her mind around that.

She glanced at the clock. Only twenty minutes left. Maybe she should flip a coin—if she could figure out *how* to flip a coin for multiple-choice questions. Maybe heads on the desk—*A*, tails on the desk—*B*, heads on the floor—

Liz felt a tap on her shoulder. "The principal needs to see you right away," Mr. Beck said softly. "Take your things."

Liz grabbed her backpack. She knew everyone was staring at her as she made her way to the door. They were probably all trying to figure out why honor student Liz Ortecho was getting called to the principal's office.

Why *would* Ms. Shaffer call her out of class? she wondered as she hurried down the hall. It had to be something big. She swung open the office door—and saw Sheriff Valenti lounging against the long counter that divided the room. His mirrored sunglasses hid his eyes, and his face was expressionless as usual.

"Sheriff Valenti needs to ask you a few questions," Ms. Shaffer said.

Liz jumped. She hadn't even realized the principal was there. The second Liz entered the room, her eyes had locked on Valenti.

"Let's go." Valenti pushed himself away from the counter and headed out the door. He didn't say a word as Liz followed him down the hall, out the main doors, and over to the parking lot. He didn't say a word as he opened the back door of his car for Liz or as he slid behind the wheel and started to drive.

Liz stared at the back of Valenti's head through the metal grill separating the front and back seats. She knew he was playing some intimidation game with her—and it was working. He was freaking her out. Had he found out what really happened at the cafe? Did he know Max healed her? Did he know *everything*?

Make him tell you what he knows, Liz coached herself. Don't volunteer anything. Don't start talking just to fill the silence. That's exactly what he wants.

She leaned her head against the seat, trying for a bored expression. She felt as if any word she said, any tiny gesture she made, could put Max in danger.

The air in the car smelled like cigarettes, and plastic, and sweat, and something medicinal. She wanted to crack the window, but she doubted that windows in police cars rolled down.

Valenti pulled into the parking lot of a small mustard yellow building near the edge of town. He got out of the car and closed the door with a quiet click. Liz almost wished he'd slammed it. At least then he'd seem human. Instead he was an ice man, totally in control. She knew she couldn't play him the way she had Elsevan DuPris.

He opened her door and started across the parking lot. Liz scrambled out and caught up with him. She lengthened her stride until it matched his. They walked across the parking lot and through the building's glass double doors side by side. She wasn't going to walk three paces behind him like a pathetic little puppy dog.

As they walked down a long hallway covered with ugly specked linoleum Liz tried to remember every detail of the story she told him at the cafe. She needed to be able to repeat it back to him today without slipping up.

Valenti stopped abruptly and swung open a door on the left. He stood back and let Liz enter the room first, then closed the door behind them.

Liz couldn't stop herself from giving a tiny gasp as she stared around the windowless room. A morgue. She was standing in a morgue. Liz had seen way too many cop shows not to recognize the stacked rows of metal drawers along one wall.

Oh, God. This wasn't about Max. She was here to identify a body. *Who?* her mind screamed. *Who is it?*

Valenti brushed past her and strode along the wall. He grabbed the handle of one of the drawers and slid it open. The sound of the tiny metal wheels rolling in their tracks sent a chill through Liz.

"I want you to see this," Valenti said, his voice calm and cool.

There was a body stretched out on the cold metal of the drawer. A plastic sheet covered it from head to toe, but Liz knew if she walked over there, Valenti would pull back that sheet, and she would have to look. She didn't want to. She didn't. If she looked, it would be real. It would be someone she knew.

Tears filled her eyes. When Rosa died, Liz had never seen her body. She could never bring herself to look, even to say good-bye. Now she had no choice. Whose body was this? Why wouldn't Valenti just tell her what had happened?

Who is it? Liz's feet moved toward the drawer. *Papa? Mama?* She couldn't stop herself from going over there. She couldn't stop herself from looking down at the body. She couldn't see much through the plastic, but she could tell that the corpse wasn't anyone she knew.

White-hot fury ripped through her. She whirled toward Valenti. "How could you do that to me? You let me think that . . ." She couldn't finish. If she said one more word, she knew she would start crying. And she wasn't going to give Valenti the satisfaction.

Valenti didn't answer. He took the top of the plastic sheet in both hands and pulled it halfway down. "What do you make of the marks on this man?" He sounded as if he were just making casual conversation, as if he had no idea he'd just put her through the most terrifying moments of her life.

Or as if he didn't care.

Liz stared at Valenti. She saw her own face staring back at her from the mirrored lenses of his shades. She felt as if she had fallen into some strange dream. Nothing made sense. Valenti was asking her to help him study a stranger's corpse? Why?

"The marks," Valenti repeated.

I have to do this, she thought. It's the only way I'm going to get out of here. She slowly lowered her eyes to the corpse. The first thing she saw was two handprints on the man's chest—iridescent silver handprints. She knew that if she placed Max's hands over those marks, they would be an exact match.

If he can heal with a touch, can he kill with a touch?

I guess I have the answer to that question, she thought. Sour bile rose in her throat.

"I . . . I've never seen anything like them before," Liz stammered. She needed time to think, time to figure out what to do. Maybe Max had a good reason for killing this guy. Maybe the guy was attacking him or something.

She forced herself to look at the corpse's face. The man looked about her father's age. His brown eyes stared vacantly at the ceiling. His lips were frozen in a grimace of pain.

Liz gagged. How could there be a good reason for killing this man? For killing anyone?

"That's interesting," Valenti said. "Because my son, Kyle, mentioned that he had seen similar marks on your stomach."

"He was wrong. It was just a temporary tattoo." She ripped her shirt out of her jeans and held it up. "See. No marks." She smoothed the shirt back over her stomach.

The handprints had been fading a little at a time. If Valenti had brought her in one day earlier, she wouldn't have been able to back up her story.

"Can we go now?" Liz asked. It came out sounding a little too much like a plea, but she couldn't help it.

Valenti ignored her. "I've seen marks like this before," he said. "They are made by the touch of a particular race of alien beings."

Liz's mouth dropped open. "You believe in aliens?"

What had happened to her nice, orderly world? The world ruled by the periodic chart? A week ago the only people who believed in aliens were tourists. Suckers who would go gaga over a photo of a melted doll. Now *she* had absolute proof that aliens existed. And the sheriff—Mr. Ice Man—was telling her he believed in them, too.

Valenti reached up and slid off his sunglasses. He shouldn't have bothered, Liz thought. His eyes were a cold gray that revealed nothing of what he was thinking or feeling.

"I am going to tell you something that I have never told a civilian—not even my own son," Valenti said. "But you're a smart girl, and you can help me. I am an agent for an organization called Project Clean Slate. Our purpose is to track down alien beings living in the United States and make sure that they pose no threat to the human population."

Liz gazed at him, trying to ignore the emotions rushing through her. Max killed someone, Max is an alien, Max is dangerous. Max loves me.

"This organization was formed in 1947, the year of the crash. That was the year we realized that aliens exist, aliens with the technology to travel to another galaxy."

"But everyone knows that UFO was a downed weather balloon," Liz said weakly.

"Don't play games with me, Ms. Ortecho," Valenti answered. "I know you've had contact with an alien. I suspect this alien somehow survived the 1947 crash, perhaps as a child who was still incubating. And I want to know what you are going to do about it."

Liz shook her head. "I don't know what you—"

"The alien who healed your gunshot wound killed this man," Valenti interrupted.

"I wasn't shot. I fell. I broke a bottle of ketchup." I wish that story were true, Liz thought. I wish I could go back to living in the safe little world where I knew all the rules, and there were no real surprises.

"That alien will kill again," Valenti continued. "Can you live with that? I saw your face when you thought it was someone you loved lying under this sheet. If you continue to protect the alien, one day soon someone will be standing right where you are, identifying the body of his mother, his father, his sister, or even his child.

"You can stop that from happening. All you have to do is tell me where to find the alien."

Liz took a deep breath. Then she pulled the sheet up so that it covered the dead man's face.

"I don't believe in aliens," she said.

Liz stood in the parking lot and stared at the school. She felt as if she'd been picked up by a tornado, viciously whipped around, and then set back down in exactly the same place she started.

She couldn't believe it was only lunchtime. Less than two hours ago she'd been worried about a history test. She started for the quad, then made a sharp right and headed for the main building. She needed a quiet place where she could sit down by herself and think. Think about what she was going to do.

Keeping Max's secret was probably saving his life. But if Max was killing people . . . Those words just didn't go together—Max and killing—but Liz forced herself to continue the thought. If Max was killing people, Liz had to do whatever it took to stop him. Which meant turning him in to Valenti.

Liz pushed her way through the double doors and started up the stairs. She'd go to the bio lab. Maybe it would help her think precisely and dispassionately, like a scientist. Whatever decision she made could have life-threatening consequences.

As Liz approached the lab she heard someone moving around inside. Damn. She really needed to be alone right now. Who had discovered her favorite place to escape? She peeked inside.

Max was sitting on one of the high stools at their lab station.

Liz stepped back and leaned against the wall. Maria would probably call this a sign from the universe, she thought. But what does it mean?

She so wanted to believe that she could trust Max. But he had been keeping a secret from her all the years that she'd known him. A huge secret. And she'd never suspected.

What if he was still hiding things from her? What if everything he told her at his house was lies—just different lies? What if humans were like lumps of meat to him? What if killing a human was like eating a hamburger or something?

"Everything's going to be all right," she heard Max say softly.

Wait. Did he know she was out there? Had he lied about being able to read her mind?

"I know you're not feeling well, but I'm going to fix you up."

Maybe there was someone in the room with him and she didn't notice.

Liz edged up to the door again. She saw Max crouching next to the mouse cage. He opened the cage door and gently took out Fred, the little white mouse. "You're going to be just fine," he murmured soothingly.

He brought his cupped hands to his chest and cradled the mouse against him. Liz could see the shocking blue of Max's eyes from all the way across the room. A moment later he returned Fred to his cage. The mouse jumped on the exercise wheel with a squeak and started to run.

Liz felt tears sting her eyes. That had to be one of the sweetest things she'd ever seen. And Max didn't know anyone was watching. He wasn't trying to fool anyone. He wasn't trying to trick Liz into keeping his secret—he didn't even know she was there.

He put himself in danger when he healed me, Liz reminded herself. He could have let me die. But that wouldn't be Max. That wouldn't be the sweet, wonderful guy who had been her friend since the third grade.

There was no way Max was a killer. No possible way.

Max closed the cage door and latched it. "No need to thank me," he told Fred. "I'll send you a bill."

He heard a soft scuffling sound behind him and turned to see Liz standing in the doorway. Her aura was rimmed with gray. He could practically feel waves of cold coming off it. Something was very wrong.

"What happened?" Max asked.

"I need to talk to you, but not here," Liz said.

"I have my car," Max answered. "Are you all right?"

"Yeah. Let's just go. The bell is going to ring soon."

Max grabbed his backpack and led the way out to his car. "Do you want to hit the doughnut place?" he asked as they climbed in. "That's where Michael always goes when he can't handle class."

Liz's face paled a little. "No. I don't want to go anywhere that I can even smell food."

"Okay, then." Max pulled out of the parking lot. "We can go to the bird sanctuary. Bitter Lakes is only about twenty minutes away. I've been there with my dad. He keeps saying he was a bird in a previous life."

Max wanted to ask Liz about a million questions on the way there, but it was obvious she was too flipped out to talk.

When they arrived, he reached across Liz and popped open the glove compartment. He rummaged around until he found a package of stale saltines. "These are so old, they don't really qualify as food anymore. We can feed the ducks while you tell me . . . whatever it is you have to tell me." Max always found it easier to talk if he had something to do at the same time.

Liz took the crackers and climbed out of the car. Max followed her over to the edge of the pond. "So," he said.

"So," she repeated. "So, Max, I found out something really important. Something you need to know. I've been trying to think of some good way to break it to you, but there is no good way."

She threw a cracker into the pond, and three ducks started a fight over it, quacking and flapping. "Sheriff Valenti is part of an organization called Project Clean Slate, which tracks down aliens. I don't know exactly what he does when he finds them, but he thinks aliens are a threat to humans, so whatever he does can't be good."

Liz took a deep breath and finally met Max's gaze.

Max felt as though she'd just shot him. He dropped down in the damp dirt near the edge of the pond. His legs felt weak and boneless. Max, Isabel, and Michael had spent hours talking about *them*, about what *they* would do if they ever discovered the aliens. But it felt a lot different now that the vague *they* was a real organization, with a real name. And that one of *them* was very close to finding Max, his sister, and his best friend.

Liz sat down next to him. "Are you all right?"

"Does Valenti know the truth about me?" Max asked in a strangled voice.

"No. Kyle told him about the silver marks on my stomach. Valenti says he knows they were made by an alien. But I didn't tell him anything," Liz answered.

Kyle saw Liz's stomach? Max felt a stab of jealousy. He told himself to get over it. Now was definitely not the time.

"There's more. Valenti brought me down to the morgue. He showed me a man's body with the same silver marks on its chest. He said . . . he said the same alien who healed me killed the man."

"I didn't—," Max began.

Liz ran her hand lightly down his arm. Max could feel her touch all the way down to his bones. "I know you didn't do it, Max," she said. "I know you could never kill anyone."

There was no trace of deceit in her aura. She meant what she said absolutely. She knew the truth about him, the truth he thought he could never reveal to any human, and she still trusted him.

Suddenly the rest of what Liz had said hit him. "Valenti took you to the morgue? That's so sadistic. If he did that to me, I would have been sure one of my parents had gotten killed or something."

"That's exactly what I did think. It's what he wanted me to think," Liz said. "I guess he figured I'd break down and tell him everything."

Max still couldn't believe she hadn't broken down. "That man he showed you has to be the guy I tried to heal at the mall. He had a heart attack. I tried to save him—I was making it look like CPR—but I was too late."

Liz nodded. "The handprints looked the same size as yours."

"How did you know . . . how did you know I didn't kill him?" With all that evidence, how could she still have believed in him? Max thought he would only find that kind of trust and loyalty from Isabel and Michael. He never imagined it could come from an outsider.

Liz met his gaze, and he thought he saw tears shining in her eyes. "I wasn't sure," she admitted. "I . . . I thought you might have done it. I'm sorry, Max. So much has happened so fast. I'm really sorry."

"It's okay. It's okay." Max wanted to wrap her in his arms and comfort her. But he wasn't sure it would be comfort. Just because she didn't think he was a killer didn't mean she wanted him touching her.

"What convinced you?" he asked.

Liz gave a snort of laughter. "A mouse. I saw you heal Fred in the lab. And I realized that someone who cared so much about a little mouse life could never be a murderer."

Her expression turned serious. "I shouldn't have

needed the mouse as proof, Max. I've seen you do hundreds of kind, good things over the years. You always know when someone is hurting, and you always try to help. You're the best guy I know. Really."

Max felt as if someone had reached into his chest and squeezed his heart. He'd never guessed Liz gave him a thought when they weren't working on one of their lab experiments. But she had noticed things about him, and she cared about him. He could see it in her eyes, hear it in her voice.

He grabbed a handful of crackers and threw them into the pond. He didn't know what to say.

"Do you remember anything about the crash?" Liz asked. "I know I freaked out when you tried to talk to me about it before, but I'd like to hear it now if you want to tell me."

"No. I wasn't even born yet—that's probably why I survived. I was in some kind of incubator when the ship went down." Max picked up a stick and started poking a row of holes in the dirt. "The first memory I have is of breaking out of the incubator pod and being in a big cave. I was about seven years old—well, that's how old the social services people thought I was, anyway, even though I'd been in the pod for a long, long time."

Liz picked up another stick and started drawing petals and stems on the holes Max made, turning them into flowers. She shook her head. "You must have been so scared. What happened to you? How did you make it out of the desert all alone?"

"I wasn't alone." Max hesitated. He'd spent so

107

many years not talking about this. He'd been the one who made Isabel and Michael swear they would never say a single word about their past to anyone. But Liz had gone to the mat for him, and she deserved the whole truth. Not just about him—about all of them.

"Isabel was with me—we shared the pod," Max said.

Liz nodded. "I wondered if she was, you know, because she's your sister."

"We picked a direction and started walking. We lucked out. We ended up at the highway just as Mr. and Mrs. Evans were driving back into town. They picked us up and took us home, and we never left.

"I don't know why they fought so hard to keep us. Two kids who couldn't speak English, who couldn't speak *any* language. Kids who didn't know how to use a toothbrush or a toilet. Kids who had been found wandering naked along the highway."

Max hurled his stick away. He hadn't thought about all this junk for so long.

"Our parents—our adoptive parents—were amazing," he continued. "They took turns teaching us at home until we were ready to start at Roswell Elementary."

"You must have learned fast. In third grade you knew the answer to every question the teacher asked. I still remember," Liz said.

"You still remember because you're so competitive. You didn't like anyone else getting points from Ms. Shapiro," Max teased. "But it's true. Isabel and I were both pretty much able to absorb information immediately. When our parents read us a book, we could always recite the whole thing back to them after hearing it just once. I guess we have really good adaptive skills. I think our systems, and our bodies, patterned themselves after what they found here."

"Wow." Liz shook her head. "I guess you don't have to spend much time on homework."

"Not really," Max admitted. "But my parents are always bringing home books—a lot of their law books, some medical books and stuff. They don't let me slack off."

He grinned, thinking of his dad's constant, good-natured nagging. What would his life be like if the Evanses hadn't found him?

It would be like Michael's life, he realized suddenly. Bouncing from foster home to foster home, never feeling like you belonged.

"Did you understand what you were?" Liz asked. "I mean, did either of you know where you came from?"

"No, at least not at first," Max said.

"I can't even imagine what it must have been like for you," Liz said. "I have this huge extended family right here in town. I know everything about them—and they know everything about me. And it doesn't stop there. At bedtime my parents used to tell me stories about my ancestors."

Liz stared out at the lake. "You know, in Spanish there are way more verb forms you can use to talk about the past than the future. I guess that shows how important the past is to my family."

She turned to Max. "I wish I could give you some

of my history. Then you wouldn't feel so lonely on this . . . world."

"It got easier when I started school," Max said. "Because I met Michael, and we both realized pretty quickly that we were . . . alike."

Liz's eyes widened. "Michael? He's a . . . one of . . . He's one, too?"

"You can say it. A-li-en," Max answered. "I don't think there's a politically correct term. We don't even know what planet we're from, so we don't know what to call ourselves. And yeah, Michael is one, too."

He frowned a little. He hadn't meant to tell her about Michael. But somehow it just came out. He couldn't seem to keep any secrets from Liz.

"Are there more of you? Is it like this whole underground community?" Liz asked.

Max scrubbed his face with his fingers. He knew it was normal for Liz to have a lot of questions, but he was starting to feel like some kind of freak. "Just the three of us. I think. We've never seen any indication that there are others.

"When we got older, we spent a lot of time talking, trying to remember everything we possibly could. We all had these memories of another place, a place like nothing we'd seen, even in books. I think they're shared memories that people on my planet are born with—you know, like humans have inborn instincts."

"I think I saw a few of them when you let me connect with you," Liz said. "I saw a sky with acid green clouds."

"Yeah, Michael and Isabel and I all have that

memory, even though none of us has ever seen anything like those clouds."

Suddenly Max wondered what else Liz had seen during the connection. Did she know how he felt about her? He hoped not. He'd already had too many humiliating conversations with Liz. He never wanted to have the one where she said she liked him as a friend. That would make him want to shrivel up and die.

He cleared his throat. "We did some research and discovered where Michael had been found. Then we got a map and drew a circle that encompassed that spot and the place where our parents found Isabel and me. We started making searches of the area—first on our bikes and later in my Jeep. And we finally stumbled on the cave. Our cave. When we saw the incubation pods, we pretty much realized the truth about ourselves. By then we'd all heard the story of the Roswell Incident—so we knew that the silvery material of our pods matched the description of some of the material of the debris found at the crash site."

"Do you know how the pods got to the cave?" Liz asked.

"We talked about that. We think one of our parents must have managed to hide the pods before they died."

Max knew the aliens in the ship must have been badly injured from the crash. But someone had climbed out of the wreckage and done whatever it had taken to save Max, Isabel, and Michael. Whoever it was must have loved us, Max thought. He felt his throat tighten up.

"Valenti got the facts pretty much right. He said he

thought an alien child had survived the crash," Liz said. "I don't know how he knew that."

Max felt stricken. Maybe the alien who moved them had tried to go back to the ship, tried to save the others. And maybe Valenti's organization had found that alien, captured it, tortured it, gotten information from it.

My parent, Max thought. Maybe Valenti's people hurt one of my parents.

"We've got to come up with a plan," Liz was saying. "Valenti's not going to give up. He's going to track you down, no matter how long it takes."

"*You've* already done enough," Max told her. "You kept our secret. Now you have to walk away. I don't want to put you in any more danger."

"Look at me," Liz said fiercely. Her hand touched his arm, and he could feel its warmth and smoothness. She was so beautiful, Max thought with a pang. "I am not going to just walk away. You saved my life, and I'm never going to forget that."

Relief flooded Max. He wanted Liz out of danger. He wanted her safe. But he also wanted her to help him, to understand him . . . to be with him. And she would. She wasn't going to just disappear.

"Then I guess we better go tell Isabel and Michael what you found out," Max said.

"And Maria," Liz told him. "She knows, too. We're all in this together."

And that means we're all in danger, he thought.

112

"I feel like I've been in a tornado," Max said as they pulled into the school parking lot. He exchanged a shy, tentative smile with Liz. Everything was still the same, but everything was different.

"I thought exactly the same thing when Valenti dropped me off after our little visit to the morgue," Liz answered.

That happened to her a lot with Maria—they were always finishing each other's sentences and making the same associations and connections. But Liz had never felt such a connection to a guy before.

"Are you ready to go in?" Max asked.

Liz stared at Max's eyes, his face. How come she had never noticed how handsome he was?

"Let's wait until the bell rings, then we can blend better. We don't need to get busted for cutting class on top of everything else."

"Liz Ortecho, outlaw," Max teased. But he didn't look at her, and his voice sounded flat and lifeless. He picked up the empty cracker wrapper and smoothed it out. He folded it in half, then in half again, and kept folding until it was a tiny square.

The stuff about Valenti is all starting to sink in, Liz

thought as she watched him. She wished she could come up with something to say that would make him feel better. But she knew there wasn't anything, so she just sat with him, hoping that at least helped a little.

Maybe I should hold his hand or something, Liz thought. She stared at his hand on the seat. The hand that had touched her wound, that had healed her. Could she help him feel better by holding his hand?

"Did you have a nice talk with my dad?" a loud voice called, jerking her out of her thoughts.

Liz looked toward the voice and saw Kyle Valenti heading for Max's Jeep.

The bell rang, the shrill sound blasting through the school doors. "Let's get out of here. I don't want to deal with Kyle right now," Liz said, keeping her voice low.

"Should I get rid of him?" Max asked.

"No, let's just go." They climbed out of the Jeep and started across the parking lot. Liz walked fast, but not too fast. If Kyle thought she was scared, it would only encourage him.

She heard Kyle's boot heels thumping against the asphalt as he followed them. "Interesting," he called in a snide voice. "You get pulled out of school for questioning, and then you and Max Evans take off together. This is very interesting. I bet my dad would think so, too."

Kyle's right, Liz thought. It wouldn't take a genius to figure out Liz might try to warn the alien she was protecting. And if Valenti heard about her cutting school with Max, he would at the very least be curious about Max—who he was, why Liz would run to him after the trip to the morgue.

Liz turned to face Kyle. Max moved in protectively, standing close beside her—and that gave her an idea.

"Why? Is your father some kind of pervert or something?" she asked Kyle. "Does he like to hear all the details of who is making out with who?" Liz slid her arm around Max's waist. She could feel the tension in his body, every muscle tight.

I hope he's not too freaked to go along with my story, she thought. Then she felt Max's arm loop around her shoulders. Good. "I talked Max into cutting class. We wanted to have some time alone," Liz added.

Kyle wasn't nearly as icy and controlled as his father. If she pushed him just a little harder, she could probably make him forget all about his suspicions. She'd just give him something more *interesting* to think about.

"Sometimes you just can't wait for school to end, you know? And both my parents were out all afternoon, so . . ."

"You and Evans—right. I believe that," Kyle said sarcastically.

Liz raised her eyebrows. "Well, I guess guys don't really notice other guys' bodies."

She let Kyle figure that one out for himself. She knew he got it when an angry flush colored his face. He pushed his way past Max and Liz without another word.

"I hope I didn't damage your little male ego," she called after him. She wanted Kyle to stay mad. It would keep him from thinking too much.

Max started to move away, but Liz wrapped her other arm around his waist and pulled him closer. "I have a feeling Kyle will be watching us. He's not as dumb as he looks," she told him quietly. "We should kiss or something."

"Um, if you really think we should," Max answered. His voice sounded lower than usual, huskier.

Liz understood why actors always said doing love scenes wasn't sexy. It was like she'd forgotten how to kiss. She couldn't decide what to do with her hands. All she could think about was Kyle watching them. If this didn't work . . .

Max tilted her chin back with his thumb, and she found herself staring up into his eyes. Suddenly it was a lot harder to think about Kyle. Max lowered his head, and she closed her eyes, expecting to feel his lips brush against hers. Instead he kissed the side of her neck. The unexpected sensation sent a shock through her.

His hands moved to her waist, pulling her tighter against him. Liz felt a low tremor coursing through him. Or maybe it's me, she thought. Maybe I'm the one trembling.

Max kissed his way up to her earlobe. "Do you think he's gone?" he whispered.

Who? she thought. Then she remembered. Kyle. This was all a show for Kyle. Her heart was thudding crazily. And Max's was, too. She could feel it through his shirt. His warmth, his strength.

Liz reached up and wove her fingers through

Max's hair, holding him close. "Maybe we should wait another minute," she whispered. "Just to be sure."

"This is your fault, Max." Isabel's voice shook with anger.

Max knew it would be tense with Isabel, Michael, Liz, and Maria in one room to talk about the Valenti situation. But he hadn't expected it to be this bad. He felt as if he were sitting in a minefield instead of his living room. The wrong word from any of them could cause an explosion that would destroy them all.

"If you hadn't healed her, this wouldn't have happened," Isabel cried.

Max knew she was terrified. He wanted to tell her that he would protect her from Valenti no matter what it took. But that would only make things worse. Isabel hated to admit that she was scared—it made her feel even more vulnerable or something. If he tried to reassure her, he knew she'd totally go off on him.

"You think he should have let her die?" Maria demanded. "Do you think that, too, Michael? Do you think Max should have let Liz bleed to death?"

Maria's aura usually reminded Max of a lake on a summer day—sparkling blue. Now it was more like an ocean before a storm—murky green and churning, potentially lethal.

"Do you think Liz's life is more important than the three of ours? Because it could come down to that," Michael answered calmly. Way too calmly. Michael wasn't a calm guy. He had himself under control—barely— and if he lost it, Max didn't know what he'd do.

"Look, even before Max healed me, Valenti knew aliens existed. He doesn't know anything more now," Liz said. She glanced from Maria to Michael to Isabel, making eye contact with each of them.

Max could tell she was trying to do some damage control, but he thought it might be too late. He should have told Isabel and Michael about Valenti alone. Being around humans who knew their secret was too much for them.

"Valenti does know something more now," Isabel insisted. "He knows that *you* know who the alien is. He's just going to keep hammering at you until you tell him."

"Liz would never do that!" Maria exclaimed.

"Liz would never do that," Michael repeated in a shrill voice, mocking her. "You only say that because you're too innocent to think of all the ways someone as twisted as Valenti can come up with to make someone talk."

"It's not Liz I'm worried about," Isabel told Maria. "It's you. You want to tell Valenti the truth, don't you?"

"We both promised we wouldn't—," Liz began.

But Maria interrupted her. "Yes! I want to tell him. I won't—not unless we all agree. But think about it— it would solve everything. He told Liz he just wants to track aliens to make sure they aren't a danger to humans. Once he finds out you're not going to hurt anyone, he'll leave you alone. He'll leave all of us alone."

"I have three words for you—*Project Clean Slate*. Does that sound like some Welcome Wagon to you?"

Michael demanded. "It's more like the politically correct way to say *death squad*."

"Michael's right," Liz said. "We can't—"

"I don't care what you have to say about it. You're not one of us." Isabel pushed herself out of her chair and strode over to Maria. She leaned down until they were eye to eye. "If you take one step toward Valenti, I'll know about it, and I'll kill you. I can do it, and you won't even see me coming. You'll go to sleep one night and never wake up."

"Shut up and sit back down!" Max exploded. "No one is killing anyone. You're acting as cold and vicious as Valenti."

Isabel straightened up and stared at Max. He could see tears shimmering in her eyes. "I'm sorry, Izzy," he said immediately. "I didn't mean it to come out like that."

"Don't even bother," she answered. "I knew you would side with them." She ran out of the room. A few seconds later Max heard his Jeep squealing out of the driveway.

"Nice going, man," Michael muttered as he went after her.

Max was glad Isabel wouldn't be alone. There was no way she would let him explain or apologize or anything for a while. But she would talk to Michael, and he'd stop her from doing anything stupid. Unless *she* convinced *him* to do something stupid.

"I have to go, too. I can't—" Maria's voice broke. She grabbed her purse and her jacket and bolted.

Max moved over to the couch and sat down next

to Liz. "I think that went well," he said sarcastically.

"I'll talk to Maria," Liz said. "I know I can convince her not to go to Valenti. She's just so scared that she wanted to believe we could tell him and he would fix everything."

"Isabel's scared, too—more than scared. She's been terrified of Valenti since we were little kids. He was like the bogeyman to her back then. She used to have nightmares about him and wake up screaming," Max answered. "But she won't hurt Maria. Isabel isn't that crazy."

Liz didn't answer. She just studied his face, her dark brown eyes intense. "What?" he asked.

"You risked everything when you healed me, didn't you?" Liz said. "Putting Michael and Isabel in danger must have really torn you up."

"I knew I could trust you," he murmured, staring at her. He could almost taste her skin under his lips. He could almost feel her body pressed against his. Without even thinking about it, he leaned toward her.

What are you doing? he thought. She let you kiss her today to get rid of Kyle. Period.

Then why did her eyes keep drifting down to his lips? Did she *want* him to kiss her again? It sure seemed that way. But if Max were misreading her signals, if she only let him touch her to throw Kyle off track, Max would look like a jerk. Worse than a jerk.

"Uh, I should go after Isabel and Michael," he said.

"There is a remarkable similarity in the accounts abductees have given of the medical procedures performed on them by the alien beings. Most report that hair and skin and tissue samples were taken and that small objects were implanted in various parts of the body. Many experienced a needle or drill penetrating the braincase."

Maria stumbled away from the exhibit. She couldn't read any more. She'd thought a trip to the UFO museum would make her feel better, because it would help her understand Max, and Michael, and Isabel. But it had filled her head with horrific images.

The aliens didn't see anything wrong with performing experiments on people. Want to know how a human thinks—why not just stab a needle in its brain? No need for anesthetic. And if you accidentally gave one a lobotomy or traumatized it so badly it could never have a job or a family—no problem, there are always more of them to scoop up.

Maria heard footsteps behind her. She turned around and saw Alex hurrying toward her. Finally. She'd called him more than an hour ago.

"I just got your message," he said breathlessly.

"You sounded really upset. What's up? Why did you want me to meet you here?"

"Do you believe in life on other planets?" Maria asked.

"Please tell me you didn't drag me down here to have one of your marathon finding-the-meaning-of-life conversations," Alex complained.

Maria glanced around the museum. There were a couple of tourists in earshot. She grabbed Alex by the arm, dragged him to the tiny coffee shop in the back, and sat him down at a table in the corner.

"Remember that day at lunch when you came up to me and Liz and she started talking about tampons?" Maria asked.

"Could you just pick a subject and stay with it for ten seconds?" Alex begged.

Maria opened her mouth, then shut it. Was she really going to tell Alex about Max and the others after she had promised Liz never to say anything to anyone?

She stared down at the table and traced one of the little alien heads decorating the tabletop. She ran her finger around it again and again. Its big, dark, almond-shaped eyes seemed to stare up at her accusingly.

Liz just didn't understand. She thought she could trust Max. She didn't realize that aliens don't have the same feelings and emotions humans do.

Alex reached out and pulled her hand away from the alien head. "Hey, something really is wrong, isn't it? You can tell me. What about that day at lunch?"

She couldn't handle this by herself. And for the

first time she couldn't talk her problem over with Liz. Liz was part of her problem.

"That day at lunch Liz changed the subject when you came up because something happened to her, something that we both promised to keep a secret," Maria said.

Alex leaned closer. "Is Liz all right?" he asked.

"Yeah. At least for now," Maria answered. Just get to the point, she told herself. "Last weekend Liz got shot while we were working at the cafe. Max Evans was there—and he healed her. He put his hands over the bullet hole, and it closed up. He saved her life."

"Oh, I get it." Alex slid back in his chair. "You and Liz are working on your project for Miss Dibble's class. Arlene Bluth told me she's going around asking people to borrow a quarter and telling them she'll mail it back. She's supposed to write a report on the reactions she gets and analyze what it indicates about society or something. Your project is much cooler."

"I'm not telling you this for some school project," Maria exclaimed. Her voice started rising out of control. She took a deep breath and continued. "I was there when it happened. I was holding this cloth over Liz's stomach, and I could feel the blood soaking through it. My fingers were getting all slippery, and I knew she was going to die."

Maria swallowed hard. "Anyway, he saved her. And when she asked him how he did it, he told her he was an alien." There, I said it, she thought. She felt horrible about betraying Liz's trust, but they were both in danger, and they needed help.

"You're serious. You really believe that Max is from outer space?" Alex asked.

"Max, and Isabel, and Michael Guerin," Maria said.

"Oh, right. Anyone else?" Alex joked. "How about Ronald McDonald—no one on earth has feet that big. And don't forget Elvis—everyone knows he's at least half alien."

"I'm serious," Maria insisted. She had to make him believe her. She had to. She needed someone on her side.

"You're tweaking. I feel like I should be taking you to a rehab center or something," Alex said. "But I know you never put impurities in your body."

"So you believe me?" Maria asked. She tightened her grip on his hands. If she had to hold him here until she convinced him, she would.

"I don't know. Let's just pretend I believe you and go on." Alex pulled his hands away and shoved his hair away from his face. "You know, you're not the first person who's told me a story about aliens. A friend of my dad's, an air force pilot, swears he saw a UFO. Swears it. And he's a total by-the-book military guy."

He was willing to listen. That was as soothing as a good whiff of cedar oil. Maria took her time and told him the whole story as calmly as she could, with as many details as possible. Alex didn't interrupt with questions. He just concentrated on what she had to say, his green eyes locked on her face.

"After I left Max's house, I called you and came straight here," Maria concluded.

"Do you know what other powers they have—besides healing?" Alex asked.

Maria shook her head. "Valenti and Elsevan DuPris both said the power to heal and the power to kill went together, but I don't know if that's true or not."

"If I knew for sure what their powers were, I'd say we should just try to talk to them. It sounds like all of you are scared," Alex said. "But that's the problem. Scared and freaked out plus possibly lethal abilities that we have no way to fight—that's not a happy combination."

"Valenti is the one with the information we need. He knows more about the aliens than anyone else," Maria said. She caught a glimpse of all the little alien faces on the tabletop and covered them with her purse. "We have to go to Valenti. He's the only one who can protect us."

This was the right place to come, Isabel thought. The entrance to the cave was almost impossible to find if you didn't already know where it was. It wasn't in the side of a cliff or anything—it was more of a crack in the desert floor.

Yeah, there was no way Valenti could know about the cave. If *anyone* had ever known about it, she would probably be floating in a jar full of formaldehyde somewhere right now. She shuddered at the image that flashed into her mind.

But that's what would have happened, she told herself. If any human had found our pods while we were incubating, they would have ripped us out, killing us before we even had a chance to live.

Isabel spotted Michael's sleeping bag in the back

125

corner. She picked it up and wrapped it around her shoulders. It was almost like having Michael's arms around her—the thick cloth was warm, and it smelled like him.

She wished Michael were here right now. It was easy to feel safe with Michael around. Besides, they needed to figure out what to do about Valenti—and they definitely needed to make their plans without Max and the humans. Max was totally worthless. Liz had him so turned around, he couldn't even see straight. He actually thought he could trust her.

I'll talk to Michael as soon as I get home, Isabel decided. But she couldn't go back yet. Valenti was out there somewhere. And this was the only place she was absolutely sure he wouldn't find her.

He doesn't know that Max is the one who healed Liz, Isabel reminded herself. And if he doesn't know about Max, he doesn't know about me. Nothing bad has happened. Valenti doesn't know anything.

But she didn't quite believe it. She'd always had the feeling that Valenti was moving closer and closer to finding out the truth, to finding her. When she was a little girl, she used to dream about him every night. Except in the dream he was a wolf, a wolf and Sheriff Valenti at the same time. In the dream he was always hunting her, sniffing and growling, and getting closer and closer to her hiding place.

Isabel sat down and leaned against the cool limestone wall. Maybe she could move in here. The cave was about three times as big as her bedroom. A portable CD player, a few pillows, her makeup drawer—it

126

wouldn't be so bad. She gave a choked laugh. Stacey would love that. Isabel Evans living in a cave.

She wasn't going to let Valenti do that to her. She wasn't going to hide from him for the rest of her life—just for tonight. Isabel wished she could close her eyes and go to sleep for hours, the way humans did. She just wanted to blank out for a while. But she couldn't. It wasn't time for her to sleep yet, and her body simply wouldn't shut down until the right time.

Isabel sighed, then she reached over and pulled the treasure chest from the hollowed-out spot in the wall. It had been a long time since she'd looked at the objects she and Max and Michael had found in the desert. Maybe they would help keep her mind off Valenti.

She opened the lid of the battered wooden chest and pulled out the little square of plasticlike material. She ran her fingers over the purple markings. She'd spent hours trying to decode them. She'd never told Max and Michael, but she'd secretly hoped they were a message from her mother.

Isabel didn't think much about her real mother anymore, or at least she tried not to. A few years ago she had rented the Roswell Incident alien autopsy tape. She had only been able to watch a few minutes. The sight of the small body lying on the metal tables sickened her—even before the doctors made the first incision.

Max and Michael kept telling her the whole tape could be a fake. They didn't know what their real parents looked like. They weren't even sure what they looked like themselves. Maybe their human bodies

127

were just a kind of practical adaptation to living on earth. Maybe on their own planet they would look completely different.

It didn't matter to Isabel if the tape was fake or not. From that night on, every time she thought about her real mother, that image had filled her mind, blocking out everything else.

Isabel's shoulders started to shake, and a hiccuping sob escaped her. That's what's going to happen to me when Valenti finds us. She could almost feel the cold metal underneath her, the cut of the knife.

She shoved herself as deep into the corner of the cave as she could. She pulled her knees to her chest and gathered the sleeping bag tight around her. "You're safe here," she whispered. But she couldn't stop another sob from ripping through her.

She heard a scrabbling sound. She jerked up her head and saw a pair of long, jean-clad legs sliding through the entrance to the cave. A moment later Michael jumped down onto the cave floor.

"Hey, Izzy Lizard," he said.

Michael crossed the cave with long strides and wrapped his arms around her. He rocked her back and forth, holding her tight against his chest.

Isabel clung to him. She finally felt safe. Safe . . . and kind of embarrassed. "I—I'm sorry," she stammered. "I c-can't stop crying."

"I've seen you cry before," he told her. He rubbed his hands up and down her back, soothing her with his touch. "You cried more than this that time I flushed your doll down the toilet."

128

"I'm getting your shirt all wet."

"You hate this shirt." Michael used the corner of his worn flannel shirt to wipe the tears off Isabel's face. "You can even blow your nose on it if you want to. That's how much I care."

"No thanks." Isabel grabbed a Kleenex from her purse and wiped her nose. Then she pulled out her compact and studied her face. Her skin looked red and blotchy. She brushed on a little powder.

"Feel better?" Michael asked.

"Feel stupid."

"Don't worry about it." He smoothed her hair away from her face, his big hands gentle. "You've done much stupider things."

Isabel slapped his shoulder. "Thanks."

Michael nodded. "Let's get out of here. Max must be flipping out."

"He deserves it. Can't we just stay here tonight?" Isabel didn't think she was ready to leave the cave, even with Michael.

"There's only one sleeping bag—and it's mine. Come on. I'll stay at your house tonight if you want."

"Will you sleep in front of the door of my room—like a big watchdog?" She smiled at Michael. It felt good to do something so normal. She'd been practicing her flirting skills on him since she was a little girl.

"I was thinking more like the couch," Michael said. "But maybe we can work something out. Would you be willing to mow my backyard?" He pushed himself to his feet and stretched his hand down to Isabel.

She let him pull her up and guide her across the cave floor. She climbed up on the rock she used to reach the mouth of the cave. Then she hesitated. "He's out there somewhere."

"He's not going to hurt you. If he tries, he's going to have to get through me," Michael promised.

Isabel knew she had to leave the cave sometime, and she'd much rather do it with Michael by her side. "Let's go."

Isabel hauled herself out of the cave. Michael scrambled up a second later. They began the long walk back to the Jeep, and Isabel pulled off the tarp they used for camouflage. They always parked it some distance away from their cave as a precaution. She handed Michael the keys and jumped into the passenger seat. "You drive, okay?" she asked. She just couldn't handle it right now.

"Sure." Michael climbed behind the wheel and backed the Jeep out of the rocky overhang where they hid it. Isabel could hear the mesquite bushes crunching under the tires as they drove back toward the highway.

"How did you get out here, anyway?" she asked.

"Hitched."

"Are we leaving tracks?" she asked. She'd never thought of that before. Were they leaving a trail that could lead Valenti to their cave?

"Too dry out here," Michael answered. "Valenti's just a man, you know. You act like he has superhuman powers or something. If he gets too close, we'll take him out."

She glanced over at Michael. He wasn't kidding.

"What about Liz and Maria?"

Michael didn't answer for a moment. "I think Max is right about Liz. If she was going to talk, she would have done it when Valenti showed her the handprints on that guy's body. But Maria . . . I don't think she wants to hurt anyone, but she's scared. And that makes her unpredictable."

"She practically said she was going to go to Valenti," Isabel reminded him.

"I bet Liz can handle Maria," Michael said as he swung the Jeep onto the highway. "But if she can't—"

The long wail of a siren cut him off. Isabel's eyes jerked to the rearview mirror. She saw the flashing blue lights of the sheriff's car, and her heart slammed into her ribs. "It's Valenti." She knew he was out here. She knew he would track her down.

Michael pulled over to the side of the road.

"Don't stop. Are you crazy?" Isabel cried.

Michael reached over and grabbed her hand. He squeezed it hard. "I was probably speeding or something. You've got to get a grip. Don't let him see how scared you are."

Isabel tensed as the sound of Valenti's boot heels grew louder. She couldn't bring herself to look over at him when she heard him stop by Michael's side of the Jeep.

"I need you to step out of the car, please," Valenti said, his voice low and even. "Both of you."

What happened to her? Ever since Isabel had stormed out of the house, Max had been able to feel her fear, strong and constant, like a headache. But about an hour ago he'd experienced something more like a hammer to the forehead. A shot of pure terror. He knew something horrible had happened to her.

I hope Michael found her first, Max thought. He couldn't stand the idea of Isabel going through something so terrifying alone. If Michael didn't find her, he would have come back here, Max told himself.

So where were they? He'd expected Isabel to come slamming back into the house a couple of hours after she left—maybe with a new dress or a pint of Ben & Jerry's that she would refuse to share with him. That's what she usually did when she had a fight with him or their parents.

Well, maybe he hadn't *expected* that to happen. It wasn't like he and Isabel had a fight about whose turn it was to wash the dishes. But he'd hoped, he'd really hoped.

"Denial's not just a river in Egypt," he muttered. It was something his mom always said. Max and Isabel were always making fun of her because she had a saying for everything. They'd even made up this game. One of them would come up with a situation, and the other one would have to come up with what Mom would say.

Max glanced at the clock. It was after two in the morning. What could possibly have happened that would stop Isabel from making it home? All he could feel from her was terror—nothing else, no hints about where she could be. He'd called a few of her friends, casually asking if she was there, but he wasn't surprised when they all said no. Izzy was popular. She had a billion more friends than Max. But they were all sort of surface, let's-hang-out-at-the-mall friends, not people she would go to if she had a problem. The only humans Isabel really trusted were their parents.

Man, Isabel, would you just come home already? Max thought. He shouldn't have yelled at her. She was already so freaked, and he'd made it worse.

He could take Dad's car and drive around. Maybe if he went in the right direction, the feelings from Isabel would get stronger. That way he'd be able to track her down. It didn't usually work like that, but Max had to *do* something. If he stayed in his room one more second, he'd go nuts. His parents would find him curled up in the corner, whispering to himself.

Max grabbed his key ring off the dresser. He decided to go out the window. His dad had X-ray hearing—if Max tried to go out the front door, he'd get busted. Luckily they thought Isabel was already home for the night. He didn't think he'd be able to find an excuse for what he was doing sneaking out after midnight. At least not one that would pass his dad's bull detector.

He slid out the window and hopped into the backyard. He trotted to the low side gate and vaulted over it. As he headed to the driveway he heard his Jeep driving down the street. He'd spent so much time working on the engine, he knew the sound by heart.

Max spun toward the sound. He felt some of the tension drain out of him when he saw that Isabel and Michael were both in the Jeep—until they pulled into the driveway and he saw their faces. All Isabel's lipstick and stuff had worn off—she never let that happen. And Michael's mouth was set in a hard line.

"What?" Max demanded.

"Valenti picked us up," Isabel answered.

"*What?*" Max exploded.

"He was just doing his usual harass-anyone-under-twenty crap," Michael explained. "But it scared the hell out of both of us."

Michael shot a glance at Isabel. Max gave a small nod, signaling that he had picked up on the fact that Isabel was seriously flipped out.

"I think . . . I think he could tell there was something wrong," Isabel stammered. "I was acting way too scared for someone . . . who got stopped for speeding, especially because I wasn't even driving."

Max could see the muscles in Isabel's throat working as she struggled to keep from crying.

"You were fine," Michael told her. He took off his jacket and wrapped it around her shoulders.

That's when Max realized she was trembling.

Isabel shook her head. "I made him suspicious. I messed up."

"He probably just thought you were worried you'd get grounded for showing up at home so late," Max said. He didn't really believe it. No one looking at Isabel right now would believe it. But he had to say something. The haunted expression on his sister's face was tearing him up.

Isabel wrapped her arms around herself. "Maybe, maybe you're right," she mumbled. "But we aren't safe for long. Valenti's going to find out about us, I know it. We have to leave town tonight, and we can't ever come back."

"If we bolt, then he'll really be suspicious. We'd end up with every Project Clean Slate agent out there searching for us," Max argued. "Besides, Mom and Dad would be devastated. They'd never get over it."

And I would never see Liz again, he thought. Something was building between them, and he wanted to be around to see what it was.

"Mr. Hughes would probably have a party if I took off," Michael muttered. "But Max is right. It wouldn't be smart."

"If we stay, we have to do something about Maria. She's going to tell Valenti everything—you saw the way she looked at us. And Liz won't be able to stop her," Isabel insisted. "We're not going to be safe as long as any human knows our secret."

Safe. Max knew how important it was to Isabel to

feel safe. He wasn't sure if she ever really had. But he couldn't let her hurt Liz or Maria.

"Liz is Maria's best friend," he said. He tried to keep his voice emotionless. He didn't want Isabel to think he was about to go off on her again. "They've known each other since they were little girls. I'm sure she'll be able to convince Maria to keep quiet."

"You have a lot of confidence in Liz," Isabel said. She didn't sound happy about it.

"So should you. Valenti came down on her hard, but she didn't tell him a thing," Max reminded her. "I want us all to agree that we leave Liz and Maria alone."

Isabel didn't answer. Michael was looking anywhere but at Max.

"Come on," Max urged.

"Okay," Michael said finally.

"For now," Isabel added.

I don't believe it. Maria told Alex. Liz could tell just by looking at his face.

Maria and Alex were waiting for Liz by her locker, and it was clear they weren't just hanging out, killing time before the first bell. They obviously had something important to say to her. "Hi, guys." Liz just wasn't ready to have this conversation. She acted really caught up in dialing her locker combination. When she pulled down the lock, it wouldn't open. She'd screwed up the combination somehow.

"We need to talk to you," Maria said. "I told Alex

everything. I know I promised you I wouldn't, but I was wrong. This whole *situation* is too big and too dangerous for the two of us to handle alone."

She sounded so stiff and formal, like she'd stayed up all night rehearsing. Liz stopped fiddling with her lock and studied her friend. Maria definitely spent last night doing something besides sleeping. Her eyes had dark smudges under them, and her complexion had a grayish tint.

"I wish you had at least called me first," Liz answered. "I left you about a hundred messages. I even stopped by your house, but no one was home."

"I know. I'm sorry. I . . . I'm sorry," Maria said again. "That's all I can say. But I don't think I did the wrong thing."

At least she's not making a speech anymore, Liz thought. Liz usually would have felt totally angry and hurt if Maria told a secret they agreed to keep. But she'd seen how scared Maria was yesterday. And Isabel did threaten to kill her. That was enough to make anybody break a promise.

"It's okay," Liz said. She turned to Alex. It was so weird to have him standing there all quiet and serious. He usually talked practically nonstop. "So now that you know, what do you think?" she asked.

"I think none of us really knows what we're dealing with—and that's dangerous. We don't know what powers they have. We don't know what their agenda is. I don't think we can just assume they are exactly what they appear to be. I think the three of us have to go to Valenti and tell him what's going on."

"No!" Liz cried. "You sound like your father, you know that? Talking about agendas and powers. We don't know what they are—so let's kill them. Maybe you *should* go into the military. I think you'd be great at it."

Alex winced. Liz knew she'd said pretty much the most hurtful thing possible. But it was true. "Look, you're both forgetting that you *do* know Max, and Michael, and Isabel. Maria, you especially. You've known all of them since we were little. They're still the same people they were—"

"They aren't people," Maria interrupted. "And Isabel never threatened to kill me in elementary school."

"And we can't be sure that they haven't just been playing us, showing us only what they want to show us," Alex added.

Liz felt like screaming at them both. She couldn't believe how stupid, and prejudiced, and horrible they were being. You felt practically the same way after Valenti got through with you yesterday, she reminded herself.

"I understand how you feel. I do," Liz told them. "Yesterday I was half convinced I should tell Valenti everything, more than half convinced. But then I saw Max heal one of the mice in the bio lab. No one was around. He didn't know I was watching. If Max has been playing us, why would he bother to save some stupid little mouse?"

"The mouse wasn't in his way. You and Maria are," Alex answered.

"What are you talking about?" Liz demanded.

"The mouse wasn't any threat to him," Alex explained. "Why not heal it? But that doesn't mean that if he felt in danger—or even if his mission was being jeopardized—that he would have any problem killing. We just don't know, that's the problem."

"Mission? What mission? Did we just enter the paranoia zone or what?" Liz demanded. "I know Max. I trust him. I am not going to do anything that might hurt him. And neither are you."

"It's not just your decision," Maria cried. "I'm the one they don't trust—you heard Isabel say it. She's going to come after me. Why don't you care about protecting me as much as you care about protecting Max?"

Liz heard Maria's voice crack. What am I supposed to do? she thought. She was stuck in the middle between her best friend and—and what? What was Max to her, exactly? Two weeks ago she would have just said he was her lab partner and kind of a casual friend. Someone who had been in her life for years but who wasn't really a big part of it. Everything had changed so much, so fast. "Of course I care about what happens to you," Liz answered. "But you're totally overreacting. No one is going to hurt you. I promise."

"You can't promise," Maria insisted. "You don't know. After school I'm going to Valenti's office—whether you come with me or not."

"I'll go with you," Alex said quietly. "Sorry, Liz. I have to."

There's no way I can stop them, Liz realized.

Nothing I can say. What am I going to do? If I tell Max that Maria and Alex are planning to go to Valenti, I don't know what will happen. Michael and Isabel really might go after them, and I'm not sure Max could stop them.

But if I don't say anything, Valenti will come after Max, Isabel, and Michael. And he'll probably kill them.

I don't want to choose, Liz thought. How can I?

What am I going to do?

"Max, come sit with us," Liz called.

Max turned and saw Liz, Maria, and Alex eating lunch on the grass in the center of the quad. He could tell by Maria's aura that she was just as upset as she had been yesterday—maybe more. A deep gray was mixed in with the churning murky green of her aura.

But it was Liz's aura his eyes were drawn to as he walked toward them. It was filled with so many colors, it hurt to look at it. There were the sickly yellow streaks of fear and the crimson splotches her aura got when she was angry. There were gray swirls of worry and confusion. And across everything was a spiderweb of dark purple. His mother's aura had a spiderweb like that after his grandfather died. It was a sign of a deep sadness. Liz slid over, and Max sat down next to her. He didn't know what to say. Was he supposed to do the usual lunchtime talk thing— someone heard Johanne Oakley throwing up in the bathroom that morning, and now everyone thought she was pregnant; there was supposed to be a raid on Guffman High that night to steal the Olsen High mascot back; Doug Highsinger got sent home for showing up at school dressed like Marilyn Manson. He didn't know if he could pull it off.

"Uh, so, what do you guys think my next list should be?" Alex asked. "I was thinking maybe alternate uses for pennies, you know, because they're pretty much worthless, and . . ." His voice trailed off.

Alex feels the tension between Maria and Liz, Max realized. You didn't have to be able to see auras to know something was wrong with both of them. Alex's aura didn't look too great itself. It had an oily, greasy cast to it.

"How about really bad dog names?" Liz jumped in. "Names you would never want to have to yell at the top of your lungs if your dog gets lost." She sounded hypercheerful and phony, kind of like Stacey Scheinin.

Something is really wrong here, Max thought.

Liz glanced between Alex and Maria, and her toothpaste commercial smile faded. "I can't do this," she said. "I can't just sit here and—Max, Alex knows."

Max felt as if he'd been sucker punched. There was no way he'd be able to control Isabel and Michael now. No possible way.

Liz reached over and grabbed his hand, lacing her fingers with his. "I want you guys to look at Max," she told her friends. "Really look at him. He saved my life. He—"

"Hey, Max, congratulations. I didn't think you'd be able to keep Liz interested in you for a whole day."

Max tensed and felt Liz's grip tighten on his hand at the sound of Kyle Valenti's voice. Kyle circled the group and positioned himself behind Alex.

You can't get into it with him right now, Max thought. It wouldn't be smart.

"Don't get too used to spending time with her, though." He smirked down at Max.

Kyle seemed like an attention deficient type. Max figured if he didn't answer, Kyle would get bored and leave.

But Kyle kept staring him. He looked a little confused, as if he couldn't figure out why Max wasn't saying anything.

"Well, I guess you could still see Liz if you don't mind visiting her in prison," Kyle continued. "Accessories to murder don't go to juvie." He turned to Liz. "You know lying to my dad makes you an accessory, right?"

"Your problem is with me. Leave her out of it," Max ordered.

"As long as she keeps lying to my father she's *in* it," Kyle shot back. "I don't know what my dad thinks, but I figure the murderer she's protecting is you, Evans. It's not too cool hiding behind a girl."

"Kyle, you're pathetic," Maria burst out. "You came up with this ridiculous theory because you can't deal with the fact that Liz would rather hang with Max than you. Just grow up already."

A dark flush colored Kyle's face. "I bet your sister would be impressed, Liz," Kyle said. "I mean, she got arrested once, too, but it was only a little drug bust. You're going to be hitting the big time."

Max leaped to his feet and launched himself at Kyle in one fluid motion. Kyle fell to the ground with a satisfying thud. Max straddled him and slammed

143

his fist into Kyle's nose. He heard it crack and felt warm blood spurt across his fingers.

"Max, no!" Liz screamed.

But he wasn't stopping now. Kyle was going to pay for every word he'd said to Liz. Max drew back his fist and brought it down on Kyle's mouth. Then he felt hands on the back of his shirt, yanking him away.

Alex hauled him off Kyle. He grabbed Max by the shoulders and pinned him to the ground.

Max jerked his head to the side and saw Kyle wiping the blood off his face with his sleeve. "This isn't over," Kyle said. Then he turned and started to walk away.

"You're right," Max shouted. "It's not over." He tried to shove Alex away. He was going after Kyle. He was going to pound the guy into the ground.

Alex jabbed his knee into Max's chest. "You're staying here. If you go after him, you're going to end up in the principal's office and both your parents are going to get called in. Do you really want to be sitting in a room with Sheriff Valenti right now? Don't you think he'd be a little curious what this fight was about?"

Max still wanted to go after Kyle, but Alex was making sense.

"Can I let you up now? Have you regrown a brain?" Alex asked. He stared down at Max, waiting for an answer.

"Yeah, okay," Max muttered. Alex let him sit up. Max rubbed his arm and studied Alex's face. "Man, how did you do that? I didn't even see you coming— then I was on the ground."

144

"Three older brothers," Alex answered. "Big ones."

"About what you said? You were right," Max told him. "Thanks."

"We have to stand together against the Kyles of the world," Alex answered.

I need some cedar, Maria thought. She opened her purse and rooted around until she felt one of the tiny vials. She pulled it out. Eucalyptus. She tossed it back inside. Eucalyptus was for invigoration, and Maria already felt ready to jump out of her skin.

Where was Max? The last bell had rung more than half an hour ago, and he still hadn't come out. She could see his Jeep from here, so she knew she hadn't missed him.

Maria peered into her purse, searching for the vial of cedar. Ah, there it was. She jerked it out and twisted off the tiny top. She brought the vial to her nose and closed her eyes. Think of a forest filled with ancient cedar trees, she told herself. See yourself in the forest and feel at peace.

It wasn't working. Maybe Liz was right about aromatherapy. Or maybe some problems were just way too big for the smell of cedar and an imaginary forest. Maria opened her eyes—and saw Max climbing into his Jeep.

"Max, wait," she called. She trotted over. "Um, can I talk to you?" She climbed into the Jeep next to him before he could answer. She didn't want him to say no.

"What's up?" Max did a little drum solo on the steering wheel. It was totally obvious he wanted to get out of there, out of there and away from her.

"Are guys, like, born with the ability to play those drum riffs?" she asked. "Because whenever I try it, it just sounds like an elephant stampede or something. And air guitar? Forget about it."

Max glanced over at her, his lips curving in a crooked smile. "I'm living proof that it's *not* genetic."

"I forgot. Duh. For one second I forgot," Maria said. "And you know why? It's because you're not this creature out of a bad movie."

"That's a relief," Max answered.

"I'm sorry. I'm making it worse," Maria cried. "What I came out here to say was that I've been afraid of you ever since I found out . . . you know. I just kept thinking that you must see me as a gnat or a pea pod or something."

"Wait. A pea pod?" Max stared at her.

"Something—other," Maria explained. "Something that wouldn't seem like a life-form in the same, what do you call it, genus or species. You know how people eat animals and plants? They can do that because they see them as something—other. If they didn't—"

"Wait. You were afraid I was going to *eat* you?" Max cracked up.

Maria stared at him—his shoulders were shaking, his mouth was stretched open, his face was turning red.

"Well, not really, but sort of, yeah, I was sort of afraid you'd eat me." Maria broke into giggles. She giggled until her stomach hurt and tears filled her eyes. When they both started to get a grip, Max snorted, and that set them both off again.

"Okay, we have to stop," Maria gasped. She squeezed her lips shut with her fingers until she got control of herself. "Okay, okay, I'm okay. What I wanted to tell you—"

Max gave a choked laugh. Maria pointed her finger at him. "No, we're not doing that again. I just wanted to tell you that it became totally clear to me at lunch how much you care about Liz. I realized I was wrong about you, and I'm sorry."

"It's okay," Max answered. "I was totally flipped out when I first found out . . . what I was. I felt like a monster, like I should stay away from everyone but Michael and Isabel."

Maria felt a rush of tenderness and protectiveness. "You're not a monster." She reached out and brushed his hair away from his forehead, then she looked away. She felt embarrassed suddenly. She and Max had never had a single conversation that wasn't totally lightweight, and now they'd both sort of spilled their guts.

"We need to figure out what to do about Valenti," she said briskly. "Kyle's going to make him even more suspicious of you and Liz. And he won't give up until he finds out the truth—about all of us."

"I think I have an idea about what to do first," Max said. "Let me give you a ride home, and I'll tell you about it. Okay, pea pod?"

Maria smiled at him, an all-out, I'll-be-your-best-friend smile. "Okay."

"Max, you are aware that we live in Roswell, not LA?" Isabel asked. "This is a little touchy-feely woo-woo, isn't it?"

"Let's just start," Liz said.

Max glanced around at Isabel, Michael, Alex, Maria, and Liz. They stood in a circle in the center of the cave, all of them looking uncomfortable.

"I think we should all hold hands," Max said.

"Oh, please," Isabel muttered.

"Tell me again why we're doing this?" Michael asked. He sounded like a five-year-old who needed a nap.

"We're doing this because before we can come up with a plan to deal with Valenti, we have to know we can trust one another," Max explained. "It's like we're going into battle—and we have to know who is covering our backs."

Alex looped his arm around Michael's shoulders. "I already have complete faith in this Power Ranger." Michael shoved him away, but Max noticed that Michael couldn't stop a grin from breaking across his face.

Max shook his head. Michael and Alex had discovered they shared the same sense of humor. Spending much time around them could get ugly. "If we hold hands, I think I might be able to form a connection between all of us—the way I do when I'm healing," he explained.

Isabel sighed loudly. "He's never going to shut up until we do it." She grabbed Max's fingers and squeezed them as tight as she could. His sister was not a happy camper. But she was a big reason Max wanted to try to make the group connection. Isabel needed a jump start to allow her to trust the humans.

Max reached for Alex's hand. He was kind of glad Liz wasn't on his other side. Touching her might make it hard to concentrate on the whole group. When he was around her, it was hard for him to focus on anything or anyone else.

He took a deep breath and began searching for a way in, a way to connect.

Liz could hardly believe they were all in one room—well, sort of a room, a cave room—together. When she first showed up, she almost wished she had a metal detector so she could check everyone for weapons. Although that wouldn't really work for aliens because they basically carried their weapons around in their heads.

And now, now they were all holding hands. It was like the end of *How the Grinch Stole Christmas!* where all the little Whos down in Who-ville stood around and sang their song welcoming Christmas. The song that made the Grinch's heart grow.

I hope this works on Isabel's heart, she thought. But that wasn't the right attitude to go into this thing with. Liz took a deep breath and tried to let go of all her thoughts, the way she did when she made the connection with Max. She imagined all the mean thoughts and prejudices and fears slipping away, becoming unimportant.

And then she heard the music.

Isabel recognized the notes echoing off the cave walls. They were the sounds of the dream orbs. She could pick out the tone of each of their orbs in the music.

The sound of each orb alone was beautiful. But together . . . Isabel let the music fill her. There was no way anyone could listen to it and feel afraid or angry. The music took the place of all her negative emotions, filling her with a sense of peace, of rightness.

The music wouldn't sound this way if there was someone here who wanted to do harm, she realized. She heard the high sound of Maria's dream orb playing follow the leader with the lower sound of Isabel's orb. I guess this means I'm going to have to be friends with her or something, she thought. And across the circle she caught Maria smiling at her.

Maria wished she could stand there forever, listening to the music. No, not listening to it. Feeling it. It washed through her in waves, sweeping away all the garbage. The thoughts about the test she had tomorrow, the anger at her parents over the divorce, and most of all her fear of Isabel.

She was as afraid as I was, Maria thought suddenly.

The thought just appeared in her mind, and she knew it was true. An image flashed into her head of Isabel curled up in the corner of the cave, terrified that Valenti was coming after her. Maria felt a wave of sympathy. It was all an act. All Isabel's threats were just to hide how scared she was. *She was never going to hurt me.*

Maria caught a hint of cedar in the air. No, not just cedar, cedar and ylang-ylang. And cinnamon. And almonds. And eucalyptus. And roses.

It's like the music is making the perfume, she thought. Then she realized the truth. *It's all coming from us.*

Michael swayed on his feet. The music and the smells were making him sort of dizzy. He needed to go outside. He needed to be alone for a minute. It was too intense in here.

Max's plan had worked. Michael was convinced that no one here was dangerous. So couldn't this thing end? He didn't know about the rest of them, but he didn't like standing here with his guts spilling out. That's what it felt like. He stared over at Max, trying to signal him that it was time to break the connection.

As he watched, Max's aura began to glow and shimmer. It was like a liquid emerald. It wasn't clouded by any emotions. It was just a jolt of one hundred percent pure Max.

Michael felt his anxiety start to fade as he lost himself in the color. He caught a glimpse of something shining to his left. He turned and saw that Maria's aura had started to glow, too, the blue of a mountain lake.

He gazed around the circle, taking in the deep purple of Isabel's aura, the warm amber of Liz's, Alex's sunny orange, and his own brick red. We really look like a rainbow . . . , he thought. And he laughed. He felt the others laughing with him.

It's like a total multimedia event, Alex thought. He tried to come up with a word for the mix of colors, music, and scents, but nothing felt right. What he was feeling went beyond language.

Alex had never felt so connected to other people, so accepted. He didn't have any friends who had known him since practically birth, friends the way Liz and Maria were friends. He'd switched schools so many times that he hardly had any friends at all. And his brothers were all older and so different. He always felt kind of like a freak around them.

Maybe this is what it's like to have lived in one town your whole life.

He'd always wanted to have a home in a place where everyone knew him.

Max slowly loosened his grip on Alex's and Isabel's hands, allowing the connection to fade.

"Whoa," Alex muttered. "All I can say is whoa."

"Yeah," Maria agreed. "Whoa."

"I think I finally know how my dad feels at a Grateful Dead concert," Liz told them.

"If we could make that in a pill form, we could become drug lords and make a billion," Michael added.

"Thanks, Max," Isabel said softly.

"So I guess now we know we can trust everyone here." The connection left Max feeling calm and hyperalert at the same time. He felt ready to take on Valenti. "Anyone have any ideas about how to handle the sheriff?"

"Actually," Michael answered, "yeah."

"Everyone knows what they're supposed to do, right?" Max asked. In less than an hour, if everything went the way they planned, Valenti would be off their case forever.

"I rehearsed in the shower," Maria told him.

"We've been over it a thousand times already, Dad," Isabel answered. "Can we please just go back into the dance? They're about to announce the homecoming queen, and I want to be there to act all surprised and happy."

"We know our stuff," Alex agreed. "Let's go. We wouldn't want Isabel to miss the big moment, right, Michael?"

"Right. That would be horrible," Michael said.

Max caught the scent of jasmine as Liz moved past him. He followed her across the parking lot and into the gym. He tried not to stare at her, but she looked so gorgeous in that dress. All long legs, and smooth shoulders, and shiny dark hair. The green material of the dress was making him crazy. At first glance it looked really sheer, almost see-through. But it wasn't really see-through because there was some kind of lining under it.

Being around Liz was like torture. It was so much worse now that he'd kissed her. It was bad enough when he used to look at her and *imagine* what it would be like to feel her in his arms. But now that he knew, it was driving him crazy. He wished he knew what she thought about those moments in the parking lot. He felt as if every sensation were tattooed on his brain. But she could have forgotten all about it. Maybe all she remembered was that it had been a good way to get rid of Kyle.

"I have to say, I'm so impressed by the decorations," Alex said. "It was a bold move to use yellow and brown crepe paper and big autumn leaves for the homecoming dance."

Michael snorted.

"Does anyone see Stacey Scheinin?" Isabel asked. She craned her neck, trying to see over the people in front of them.

"She's right over there, crammed between two football players," Maria answered.

Isabel moved next to her. "Oh yeah. Now I see her. Good. I want a view of her face when they make the announcement that *I'm* this year's homecoming queen."

"Okay, the moment you've all been waiting for," Ms. Shaffer called from the stage at the front of the gym. The microphone whined, and she winced. "This year's homecoming queen and king are . . . Liz Ortecho and Max Evans."

Isabel stopped in midsqueal. "What?" she cried.

"Go on up there," Maria exclaimed. She gave Max a push.

"Let's go." Liz sounded as surprised as Max felt. She took his hand and led the way up to the stage. Ms. Shaffer was reading the names of their court, but Max couldn't focus. How had this happened? He could understand why Liz won. Liz was the most beautiful girl in school, plus she was totally popular, definitely one of the elite—it only made sense that she got a ton of votes. But who would have voted for *him*?

He climbed up the steps and headed over to Ms. Shaffer. Everyone in the gym was clapping and whistling. He could hear Michael and Alex hooting louder than anyone. They had to be loving this. It's not like any guy really wanted to be homecoming king.

Ms. Shaffer handed Liz a bouquet of roses and placed a dime-store rhinestone tiara on her head. Max leaned down so she could put the crown on him. Liz kissed his cheek, and he could tell she was trying not to giggle by the way her lips were vibrating.

Some love song started to play, and a spotlight hit Liz and Max, blinding him. "We're supposed to dance," Liz whispered.

Max jumped off the stage and held his hands up to Liz. She let him swing her down to his side. He felt kind of awkward. He would have loved to slow dance with Liz by themselves or even in the middle of a big crowd. But everyone had cleared a circle in the center of the gym floor so they could start off the dance alone.

Liz reached up and wrapped her arms around his neck, and her body brushed against his. Max felt as if his blood had turned carbonated, popping and fizzing in his veins. He placed his hands on her waist. He didn't try to pull her closer. We're friends, he told himself.

"I felt sort of frozen up there," he said. He thought it would help him do the friend thing if he talked. "You know, like a polar bear at the zoo. All those people watching me."

Liz chuckled. "Why?"

"Because I've always been the quiet guy," Max answered. "If a total unknown can become homecoming king, it has to be a joke, right?"

"You're not a polar bear." Liz smiled. "You're too good-looking—like you should be on *Baywatch* or something," she answered.

"Everyone still thinks I'm strange." Max knew it was true, but he didn't really care.

"They think you're quiet." Liz started playing with the hair at the back of his neck.

Wait, Max thought. What was that? Does a girl who wants to be friends play with your hair like that?

"I was thinking that we should kiss. People are going to be expecting it—since we're king and queen and everything," Liz said. She sounded like she was half teasing, but half not.

Max couldn't believe this was happening. Liz Ortecho wanted him to kiss her. "If you really think we should," he said, grateful he could speak at all.

He lowered his head and brushed his mouth against hers. Liz's lips parted, welcoming him, deepening their kiss. Max kept his eyes wide open. If he shut them, it would feel too much like a dream.

*   *   *

"Maybe I need to get contacts," Stacey told Isabel. "Because I didn't see you up there."

"You weren't up there, either." Tish jumped to Isabel's defense.

Isabel felt like she'd slipped into an alternate universe. Her *brother* had just gotten elected homecoming king, and Isabel was standing on the sidelines. Hello—what was wrong with this picture?

"They're playing our song."

Isabel glanced over her shoulder and saw Alex standing behind her. Uh-uh, she thought. Just go away, little man. I am not in the mood.

"They're playing our song," she repeated, mocking him. "Are you auditioning for a part on the new *Love Boat*?"

"Ouch," Alex answered. "Don't tell me you don't remember dancing with me right here in this gym to this song."

Why is he asking if I remember something that only happened in his dream? Is he a moron? Or has he been talking to Michael? she thought suddenly.

She noticed Stacey and Tish listening to their conversation without even bothering to pretend they weren't. "Fine. I'll dance with you."

"Your humble love slave thanks you," Alex answered. He pulled her firmly against him.

"You heard that?" Isabel asked. She had thought Alex was out of the gym that time she had made fun of him.

"Yeah, I heard," Alex said. "I also heard how you like to go into people's dreams and play little games with them."

"I'm going to kill Michael."

"Don't you want to know why your plan didn't work first?" Alex asked.

Isabel narrowed her eyes at him. "What plan?"

Alex traced the line of her dress's low back with his finger. She felt a little shiver rush through her, but she refused to be distracted. "What plan?" she repeated.

"Project Homecoming Queen," Alex answered. His fingers moved higher, sliding under her hair and rubbing the back of her neck.

Isabel felt as if she were losing the ability to think. But she forced herself to focus. "You were supposed to vote for me. Every guy in school was supposed to vote for me."

Alex leaned down and whispered in her ear, "I'm sure they would have—if Michael and I hadn't come up with a counterattack. He went back into all the guys' dreams and showed them another side of Isabel Evans."

Isabel pushed back from Alex and glared up at him. "What is that supposed to mean?"

"Let's just say most guys find a homecoming queen picking her nose sort of a turnoff."

Isabel was speechless.

Alex continued to grin at her.

He hadn't. He *had!* Isabel thought about storming off in a huff. But she was discovering that Alex had pretty amazing hands—and she kind of wanted to see what he'd do with them next.

Isabel shot Michael an evil glance. Then she rested her head on Alex's shoulder and closed her eyes.

Michael laughed. It was good for Izzy to get put in her place once in a while.

And that night hanging out with Alex had been pretty fun. They had eaten their way through every flavor of chips—Michael had dipped his in chocolate sauce—while they came up with really gross images of Isabel to put into the guys' dreams.

They had done their strategy session in the cave, not at their homes, because it turned out that Alex's dad was pretty much a jerk, too.

"Max and Liz look amazing together," Maria said. "He has that whole blond-Viking thing going, and she has that dark, dark hair and eyes." She sighed. "Isn't it romantic?"

"So a guy is sort of like a walking accessory? You just choose one that looks good with your hair? Is that it?" Michael teased. "Because if it is, you should be dancing with me. I have that dark, dark hair, and you're almost blond enough to be a Viking. I can definitely picture you in one of those helmets with the horns."

He pulled her out onto the floor. She smelled good. Sweet, like vanilla.

"Are you sure I'm not too innocent for you?"

Michael stared down at her. "What are you talking about?"

"That day at Michael and Isabel's. You said I was too innocent to know all the ways Valenti could make someone talk," Maria reminded him.

"You make it sound like I called you something horrible." Michael didn't get it.

"Innocent is like cute," Maria insisted. "A word you use for kittens."

"Well, I hate to tell you this," Michael said, "but I think you're cute, too."

Michael pulled her closer and rested his cheek on the top of her head. He heard her give a little sigh as she snuggled up against him. Just like a little kitten, he thought. A nice, soft, warm kitten. But he didn't bother telling her that.

He glanced at the clock. About twenty minutes to go before we start the plan. He felt his stomach tense.

"Are you okay?" Maria mumbled.

"Yeah." He let himself relax in the sparkling blue of her aura. Yeah, he was okay. Because no matter what happened, he wouldn't have to face it alone.

The connection Max had formed among the six of them in the cave hadn't completely broken, even though it had been two days. He could still *feel* the others around him. It was like he finally had a family. And he would do whatever it took to protect them— all of them.

Maria scanned the gym wildly. Where was Kyle Valenti? She had to find Kyle, *now*.

She spotted him near the stage and ran toward him, pushing people out of her way. "Kyle, call your dad! Someone stabbed Alex in the neck. He's out in the parking lot. Hurry!"

Kyle didn't say a word. He turned around and bolted for the pay phone against the back wall.

Half the people in the gym were trying to shove their way over to the big double doors leading to the parking lot.

"This way." Liz appeared at Maria's side. She grabbed her hand and dragged her out the side door. They ran down the hall, their footsteps echoing in the empty building. They burst out the main entrance and tore over to the parking lot.

"Let us through," Maria begged. She and Liz squeezed their way past the rows of people crowding around Alex. He sat on the ground, a dazed expression on his face.

"I thought you said he was stabbed," Liz cried.

"He was," Maria insisted. But there was no wound on Alex's throat. And the blood on his skin was already starting to dry.

"I want all of you back in the gym," a loud voice ordered. Maria didn't have to look to know that it was Sheriff Valenti. "Now," he barked.

"I guess we'd better go back," Liz said. "Are you going to be okay?" she asked Alex.

"Yeah. Go on."

Valenti pushed his way through the retreating crowd. "Do you want to tell me what's going on?" he asked Alex. "I got a report that you were stabbed, but that's obviously not what happened."

Alex pushed himself to his feet and leaned against the closest car. His legs felt a little rubbery. "I came outside because the gym was really hot. Some guy came up from behind me and told me to give him my wallet. I told him to forget it."

Valenti made a circling gesture with his hand. He obviously wanted Alex to get to the point a little faster.

"The next thing I knew, I was on the ground," Alex said quickly. "He tackled me, I guess. And then I saw the knife. The guy stabbed me in my throat. That's all I remember. Maybe I blacked out or something."

"Do you want to try to explain why you aren't dead?" Valenti asked. "There are a lot of veins and arteries in the throat, and you're not even bleeding."

"I don't know. I guess the guy just nicked me. Maybe I passed out from fear. Pretty humiliating," Alex answered.

Valenti shone the flashlight in Alex's face, studying him for a long moment. Then he moved the beam down onto Alex's throat.

"You want to tell me the rest of the story?" Valenti asked.

He saw the mark, Alex thought. He saw the silver handprint.

"I told you I don't remember," Alex answered. He wished he could see Valenti's eyes. Who wore sunglasses at night?

"Will you remember better if I bring you back to my office? We can go back there and have a nice long talk," Valenti said.

"You're not going to believe me, all right? What's the point of telling you?" Alex cried.

Valenti didn't answer. He just stared at Alex from behind his shades.

Alex sighed. "Okay, this is what happened. The guy stabbed me in the throat, and then he ran off because he heard someone pulling into the parking lot. This *other* guy came over to me, and he put his hand over the hole in my neck, and it . . . it just closed up. So are you going to take me to the mental ward now?"

"What did this *other* guy look like?" Valenti asked.

"I don't know. I mean, I was bleeding to death. That kind of had my complete attention." Alex could tell Valenti didn't like that answer, but he didn't push it.

"What about the car—what was he driving?" Valenti demanded. Alex looked at the ground, thinking. "It was an old green pickup. I saw it when he pulled back out of the lot. He turned left, heading out of town, I guess. But shouldn't you be asking me about the guy who tried to kill me?"

"Later." Valenti turned and strode toward his

cruiser. He climbed in and closed the door with a quiet click, then pulled the car out of the parking lot and turned left. Heading after the green truck.

What did I just do? Alex thought.

Max heard the high scream of a siren behind them. He glanced over at Michael. "Valenti," they said together.

"Let's see what this baby can do," Michael said.

Max tried to increase his concentration. He could see the molecules that made up the old truck spinning around them. He shoved them forward—without letting them break apart—moving the truck forward with his mind.

"You are helping me push, right?" Max asked.

"No, I'm just here for the ride," Michael shot back. "Of course I'm helping you push."

Max checked the rearview mirror. He could see the lights of Valenti's cruiser in the distance. "Well, push harder. He's gaining on us." If they didn't make it to the Lake Lee overlook before Valenti caught up to them, it was all over.

Max knew fear made it harder to move the car. He took a couple of deep breaths, the smell of the lake's salt and minerals filling his nose. He focused completely on the molecules, slamming them forward.

The truck picked up speed. Max darted a quick glance at the rearview mirror. Still okay, he thought. The truck bounced and rattled as they sped down the road to the overlook.

"Okay, let's do it," Michael yelled.

Max threw open his door. He heard Michael's door click open at the same time. The ground rushing past made him dizzy. "Don't look down," he called to Michael—and then he jumped.

Pain shot through his elbow as he landed. He ignored it. He had to concentrate on keeping the truck moving. It was harder to control the molecules from a distance, but he gave one last hard shove with his mind. The truck crashed through the fence and made the eight-story drop into Lake Lee, landing with a huge splash.

Michael ran over and pulled Max to his feet. Valenti would reach the overlook any second—and they had to be out of sight.

"How lucky are we to live so close to a bottomless lake?" Michael asked as they took off.

Max didn't answer. He wanted all his breath for running. He raced back toward town until his lungs felt like they were on fire, then he slowed to a jog.

"Tired already?" Michael asked. But Max could hear him panting.

"Thought I'd give you a chance to rest," Max answered. They kept their pace at a fast jog all the way back to the school parking lot.

Before they headed into the gym, Max ran his fingers through his hair and brushed the dirt off his pants and shirt. His jacket would hide his sweat-soaked shirt. He wiped his forehead with his sleeve.

"Aw, do you want to look nice for Liz?" Michael asked.

Max slapped the dirt off Michael's back. "We want

everyone to think we've been here the whole time, re-member?" He led the way back to the gym. In two seconds Liz, Isabel, Maria, and Alex were gathered around them.

"So did it work?" Liz asked.

"Right now Valenti should be standing at the edge of the cliff, crying about the alien that got away," Michael answered.

"Good going," Alex said.

Max could see relief and happiness swirling in all their auras. The connection between the six of them was so strong that the edges of their auras blended, forming one brilliantly colored ring around all of them.

"We did it," Max said. "It took all of us, but we did it."

Liz knew she was staring at Max, but she couldn't help it. She needed to keep reassuring herself that he was really okay. If Valenti had caught him out there in the desert, Liz might never have seen Max again. A world without Max. That was not a place she'd want to live.

Max leaned close to her. "Do you feel like getting some air?" he asked in her ear.

"You read my mind," Liz answered. She couldn't wait to be alone with Max. "We'll be back in a little while," she told the others.

"Take your time," Maria answered. Michael laughed.

I guess everyone noticed the way we were sort of all over each other on the dance floor, Liz thought as they headed outside. But so what? She didn't care who knew how she felt about Max. She didn't know exactly when it had happened—whether it was when they had sat together at the bird sanctuary and he told her about his childhood; or when he had let her connect to him, allowing her to access his uncensored thoughts; or when she had seen the deep green of his aura in the cave and felt the deep, pure goodness of him; or maybe it was watching him cure the little mouse that had done it—but somehow, somewhere she had fallen in love with him.

Max led the way over to one of the benches in the quad, and they sat down next to each other. Liz expected him to kiss her again or at least hold her hand. But he kept staring down at the ground, his expression serious.

"Is something wrong?" she asked. "Are you worried that Valenti won't believe the alien he's looking for is dead?"

"No, Michael came up with a good plan. I think it worked. Valenti's never going to be able to recover the truck, so he'll never find out no one was inside," Max answered, but he still wouldn't look at her.

Liz reached out and ran her fingers down his cheek. "I just need to touch you. I need to make sure that you're really back. I was so worried about you."

She took a deep breath. She had to tell him how she felt about him. "We've been friends for so long that I think I just sort of took you for granted. I knew you were smart. I knew you were a great guy, that you were always thinking about other people. Remember how you used to pick Maria to be on your softball team every single time?"

168

Max nodded, but something felt off, Liz thought. He seemed distracted, distant. Of course he's distracted. He just risked his life to keep Valenti away from all of us.

Liz decided to keep going. It would be a lot harder to start this conversation all over again later. "Anyway, I knew all these things about you, but I never thought about how I'd feel if you weren't around. I'd feel bad. Well, of course I would feel bad. Why is this so hard?" Liz stopped and closed her eyes a moment. "Let me just get to the point. I love you, Max."

Enough talking, she thought. She leaned toward him. It felt like forever since their last kiss. She needed to feel his arms around her.

Max stood up and shoved his hands in his pockets. "Michael's plan worked," he said, repeating himself. "But I'm always going to be in danger. There's always going to be someone out there hunting for me—Valenti or somebody else."

Liz shivered in the cold night air. She wrapped her arms around herself. She knew Max loved her, too. She'd seen it in his thoughts, felt it in the way he touched her. What was wrong? Why was he acting so strangely?

"If you get too close to me, you're going to be in danger, too," Max said in a rush. "I think . . . I think we should stay friends. Just friends."

Liz jumped up. "Max, we found a way to deal with Valenti. We did that together—all of us. If something else happens, if someone else gets close to

169

finding out the truth, we'll deal with that, too," she told him, her voice tense and urgent. "I love you. I want to be with you. Nothing else matters."

Max's arms were around her before she could say another word. He buried his face in her hair. "We can't—," he half said, half moaned. Then his lips found her mouth. They kissed, a long, passionate, heart-searing kiss.

He loves me! Liz thought giddily. He loves me, too.

Suddenly Max broke away. "No. It's more important to me to keep you safe." He stared into her eyes, his expression serious. "I'm not going to change my mind about this, Liz. It's too important." He released his urgent grip on her shoulders.

Liz stared back at him, his intense blue eyes, his rumpled hair, the line of his jaw. She could tell that nothing she said was going to change his mind right now.

Max turned and stumbled away from her.

Liz felt stunned. But she wasn't going to give up— not now that she'd finally realized how she felt about him. She and Max were meant to be together here, now—and she was going to find a way to prove it to him, no matter what.